Shamberlin,
I have enjoyed getting
to know you! I hope
this book inspires
you.
♡,
Jennifer

RUBBER BAND *Girl*

A Mother's Memoir

Jennifer Nielson

Sourced Media Books, LLC

ISBN 978-1-937458-13-3

LCCN 2012947647

Visit www.sourcedmediabooks.com

To Hadley

I am not tall.

Everyone else is just short.

HADLEY

Contents

Prologue

Every man's life is a fairy tale
written by God's fingers.

HANS CHRISTIAN ANDERSEN

Life is rarely a fairy tale. But there are lessons to be learned from those timeless characters who faced overwhelming obstacles before reaching their "happily ever afters." From Red Riding Hood's big bad wolf to Cinderella's evil stepmother to the billy goats' troll under the bridge, it is triumph over opposition that makes these stories worth telling. So it is that these seemingly insurmountable obstacles in our path are often the gateways to our happy endings.

My very own princess, Hadley, has come up against her share of trolls under the bridge. Diagnosed with Marfan Syndrome at a young age, Hadley has experienced many obstacles associated with the condition. But while Marfan's can be debilitating and even life-threatening, Hadley has seen her life as nothing but a fairy tale.

Hadley started out as an "average" baby girl, although that would be the last time that adjective could accurately describe her. Like Jack and the Beanstalk, Hadley seemed to have her own supply of magic beans: Once she started growing, she kept growing, and growing, and growing.

It goes without saying that we live in a society that promotes a certain body type—and being too big doesn't fit into that mold. Even Goldilocks knew that in order for something to be "just right," it couldn't be too big or too small. Yet, Hadley has never been bothered by not fitting into an "ideal" mold. As Hadley's body stretched like a rubber band, so did her spirit. She now exudes the bravery and confidence of a storybook hero and continues to meet her challenges head-on. In fact, my not-so-little princess loves the fact that she isn't like everyone else and has never longed to be anyone else's version of "just right."

Hadley's zest for life has become contagious and has spread to her family, her friends, and even her community. Her unconquerable attitude in the face of adversity, coupled with her passion for helping others, is as inspiring as any fairy tale ever told.

This is Hadley's story.

CHAPTER ONE

Waiting Game

Adopt the pace of nature:
her secret is patience.

Ralph Waldo Emerson

In the dim light of the restaurant, Talan's handsome face looked almost boyish, like the first time I met him in the small, Arizona bowling alley.

"Who is Mr. Tall, Dark, and Handsome?" I had asked my brother upon first laying eyes on Talan. In his green polo shirt, jeans, and Birkenstocks, he was my kind of irresistible—and I was hopelessly smitten.

Nineteen years and four children later, I was still looking at the same beautiful eyes and captivating smile. Talan and I had experienced our share of bumps and bruises; but, together, we had managed everything that had come our way. I realized that through trials and triumphs and everything in between, Talan and I had become closer than ever.

The smell of garlic and freshly baked bread tantalized my already growling stomach. Over the drone of Italian opera, Talan asked, "If we could go anywhere for our twenty-year anniversary, where would it be?"

"Europe!" I exclaimed, without hesitation. Early in our marriage, we had spent three glorious weeks backpacking through Europe. The adventure and beautiful scenery left me with an insatiable appetite for travel. As I contemplated the majesty of the Swiss mountains and the rich aromas of Parisian cuisine, I was transported back to a time when life was much . . . simpler.

"Jennifer!"

I was roused from my spell at the sound of a familiar voice. A friend I hadn't seen in years was approaching our table.

"Aimee! How are you? It has been so long!" I greeted her warmly. I loved running into old friends, and although I lived in the town I grew up in, it didn't happen as often as I would have liked.

"How are you?" she replied and then, as a shadow passed over her face, added, "And how is Hadley?"

It was a question I had heard all too often, but her sincere concern was worthy of a response. After listening to my update, she revealed that her thirteen-year-old daughter had recently been diagnosed with a debilitating health condition that had her in and out of the hospital. The unfortunate progression had forced her daughter, a passionate gymnast, to quit at the peak of her success. I struggled to hold back tears as I saw a familiar anguish in my friend's eyes that conveyed a heartache I knew too well. Their world, like ours, had been turned upside down.

After our goodbyes, my husband and I sat in silence, keenly aware of the struggles that lay ahead for my friend. Only those who have actually touched a hot stove know what it feels like. And in that moment, we were both nursing that burn. Our reality was one from which we could not escape, even for one night. Our perfect evening had taken an emotional detour; but, by the time our food arrived, the ache in our hearts subsided, and we discussed plans for a much-anticipated family trip to the mountains that weekend.

Life is full of unexpected twists. It was Hadley who had taken our lives in this unforeseen direction, turned everything I knew inside-out, and allowed me—a reluctant participant—to experience the heights of joy and the depths of sorrow. It was Hadley who filled my heart with so much love I thought it would burst.

I looked at my husband, deeply grateful to have him as my partner on this arduous journey. His support was everything. It was Hadley and I, however, who endured endless visits to doctors together. Hadley spent as much time in doctors' offices as some kids spend at the park. Our most recent appointment was one of the most significant yet.

"How has Hadley been doing?" the front desk nurse inquired.

"Wonderful!" I repeated (my standard reply). As we waited in the aptly named room, I grew increasingly nervous; visits to this specialist always heightened my anxiety. There was so much at stake. Hadley's life had already been dramatically altered; but, if her health condition were not monitored properly, her very life could be threatened. Mercifully, this reality eluded me most of the time. I had become an expert at compartmentalization, tucking painful realities away into a part of my brain that I locked away except when absolutely necessary. Visits to the doctor fell into this category. While I did my best to forget, the painful truth was always hovering on the fringes of my consciousness. I felt that familiar lump forming in my throat as the reality of Hadley's health condition overwhelmed my mind.

Looking around the waiting room, I saw other mothers dealing with similar challenges and wondered if they were feeling the same way. Having a child with health issues opens you to a new world of heartache and worry, and nothing brings that worry to the center of your attention more than an endless regimen of doctor's appointments (and, of course, the inescapable by-product—waiting).

I watched Hadley, unfazed as she scoured magazines for entertainment. The Disney cartoons playing overhead had lost their appeal long ago.

"Mom, how much longer is it going to be?" Her patience was wearing as thin as mine; but, before I could answer, a wobbling toddler knocked over by an older sibling wailed, and Hadley ran to help the crying child to his feet. It was satisfying to realize that this daughter of mine, with all of her problems, had already figured out that the best way to forget her own troubles was to help someone else in their time of need.

Hadley dwarfed the other children in the waiting room, doubling most of them in size. The question in most of their staring eyes was, "What is *she* doing at a *pediatric* doctor?" I had grown defensive of the scrutiny. Sometimes it was subtle, sometimes not. Ordering for Hadley off the children's menu or buying her a child's admission movie ticket often made me feel like I was trying to get away with something I shouldn't do. At times, I was tempted to carry her birth certificate with me so I could flash it and shout, "Look, she really is under twelve. Bug off!"

"Mom, do you want to play this game with me?" Hadley drew my attention back to one of our waiting rituals.

"Sure," I quickly answered, grateful for the distraction. We combed the hidden picture games in the *Highlights* magazine and raced to see who could find the objects the fastest. That she still enjoyed this activity on the verge of becoming a teenager gave me satisfaction—and to be honest, I enjoyed the games as much as she did. The one thing that made the appointments bearable was the large block of time it gave the two of us to spend together. As we talked and played, I saw love in her eyes. She and I were best friends, and I prayed that wouldn't change anytime soon.

I didn't expect today's prognosis to be any different from those of past visits. Long ago we had received the heartwrenching diagnosis: Marfan Syndrome, a genetic disorder of the connective tissues that results in weak ligaments. Marfan Syndrome is also called the "rubber band disease," because its most visible symptoms are extreme height, excessively long limbs, and overly stretchable ligaments; but, the disease affects the entire function of the body, impacting the heart, eyes, back, and skin most severely. It affects one in five thousand people throughout the world. As I listened to the life sentence pronounced upon my daughter, I thought my heart would stop—and my heart wasn't the faulty one.

It was in this doctor's office that we first learned that Hadley would be restricted from certain physical activities because of her health condition, especially activities like contact sports. This was a harsh reality, as

Hadley was a tomboy whose first love was basketball. Playing basketball would be off-limits, and it rocked her five-year-old world. I nearly cried when we left the office that day and she asked, "Does this mean I can't play in the WNBA?" My dreams for Hadley involved her playing the piano, dancing on stage, or becoming an accomplished singer—they certainly didn't include basketball—but even at her young age, she knew what she wanted. She was crushed to hear that her dream would never come true.

I was roused from my reflections of the past by Hadley's voice.

"Where should we have lunch today?" Hadley asked. Lunch always followed doctor's appointments, giving us something to look forward to.

"How about Top Shelf Cantina?" I suggested. Hadley agreed and went back to searching for missing objects in the magazine.

A monotone voice finally called out, "Hadley Nielson, please come back." I breathed a sigh of relief as we made our way back to our designated room. I couldn't help but be charmed by the bounce in Hadley's step. Her warmth defied the sterile surroundings. We sat in the familiar room—I on a cold, hard chair and Hadley atop the white paper of the exam table. I wondered which of us was more uncomfortable. Hadley, now twelve, was a veteran patient. She knew the drill.

I waited for the doctor with as much anticipation as Dorothy in Oz. He was like the wizard at the end of the yellow brick road with the answers to all my questions. This state of uncertainty was so familiar now; I'd been living with an unknown prospect for the future for so long. I wasn't sure I was prepared to hear the answers. While I tried to remain positive, my mind's nagging interrogation of the universe resumed: *How did this happen? How did we get here? And is there any hope of recovery?*

Chapter Two

Playing House

Be not afraid of greatness: Some are born great, some achieve greatness, and some have greatness thrust upon them.

WILLIAM SHAKESPEARE

When I gave my husband a jar of spaghetti sauce, he was over the moon. The "Prego" label declared the news. We were thrilled to be expecting our second child. We cherished being parents to our older son, Hayden, and we were ready to add another child to our family. Being pregnant was a time of blissful anticipation.

Talan and I had always wanted a big family. I had grown up with ten siblings, and Talan had four, so big families were familiar to us. As a little girl, my favorite toys were the brand new baby dolls Santa Claus would leave under the tree for me on Christmas morning. My sisters and I would giggle with delight as we cuddled our babies and deliberated on the perfect names. I played house for hours, changing diapers and feeding my "babies" from make-believe bottles. I envisioned my future babies as precious and perfect as these little dolls. Still, nothing could have prepared me for the immense love and satisfaction I felt as I held my real babies in my arms. The fulfillment I discovered in motherhood far surpassed all of my girlhood expectations.

As I watched Hayden grow into an active, gregarious toddler, my appreciation for each new stage grew too. He was so calm and easygoing—I couldn't imagine anything better than this. I wondered if I could possibly love another child as much as I loved him, but I also knew the best thing for Hayden was a brother or sister.

I asked Talan, "If you could choose, would you want a girl or a boy?" His answer was usually the same—he'd be happy either way. "Of course," I would reply. Despite the common "Daddy's girl" cliché, I think most fathers naturally envision themselves raising sons, while mothers yearn for baby girls—but since we already had Hayden, the pressure was off for Talan. Even though I knew that a mother's love transcended gender, in my heart of hearts I longed for a daughter.

Technically, Hadley had her first doctor's appointment while she was still safely nestled inside my pregnant belly. I waited anxiously for the day of the ultrasound. Sure, I wanted to know the baby was healthy, but I was dying to know: pink or blue? I begged for an early morning appointment to make the agonizing wait more bearable.

After dropping off Hayden at Grandma Nielson's for a much-anticipated day of treats and one-on-one attention, Talan and I were ready to enjoy the appointment with no distractions. Exchanging pregnancy stories with others in the waiting room only added to my excitement. "How far along are you?" "Are you having a girl or a boy?" "Do you have any names picked out?" We filled the long wait with enthusiastic chatter as my anticipation grew.

Finally, we were called into the doctor's office. "How are you feeling?" he asked as he prepared the ultrasound machine.

"Tired but good," I answered. It had been an easy pregnancy so far. In a moment, I was staring at a blank screen. My heart began to beat out of my chest, and soon the baby's profile came into view. I saw limbs, then organs. The "blink, blink" of a little heart beating brought tears to my eyes.

The doctor paused then, with a grin on his face, told me what I was hoping to hear: "It's a girl!" I was euphoric! I instantly began dreaming of her future; and from the look in my husband's eyes, I could see that he was doing the same.

Two weeks before my due date, Hadley decided she was ready to take her show on the road. Following a routine visit to the doctor, I stood up only to have my water break right there in the middle of the examination room. I immediately called Talan. "I need you to come now—it's time!" I gasped.

He was still in shock when he arrived at the doctor's office. "Is this really happening? You aren't due for two weeks."

"You better believe it," I assured him. "We are having this baby tonight!"

After a few hours of waiting, followed by a few hours of labor, Hadley Ann Nielson arrived in a blessedly smooth delivery on the evening of November 19, 1997. Hadley was a beautiful, healthy, average-sized baby girl weighing in at seven pounds, eleven ounces and measuring nineteen and three-quarter inches tall. I had yet another case of love at first sight. As I held her in my arms for the first time, I was drawn in by her trusting brown eyes that seemed keenly aware of her new world.

"Talan, isn't she beautiful!" It was more of a statement than a question.

He smiled back. "Yes, she is." Hadley had already cast a spell on us. As I examined her long, delicate fingers wrapped around my pinky, I wondered if she'd learn to play the piano, love music, sing, or dance. I knew Talan was wondering what sport she'd most love to play. What we shared was an unconditional love for Hadley and a desire for her to live a life of endless possibilities.

When Hayden came to visit his new baby sister in the hospital, he suddenly seemed enormous. Where had my little boy gone? It was our first time together as a family since Hadley had been born. He crawled in the hospital bed with us and began analyzing this new foreign creature in my arms. "Mommy, are we going to leave her here?" I shook my head no, and he stared back at me with more than a little disappointment. He was too young to understand, so I offered the only reassurance I knew would make it better—a chocolate chip cookie brought by a previous well-wisher. In no time he devoured the cookie and forgot his worries.

The pile of crumbs I discovered in the hospital bed as I was preparing to leave was a sweet reminder of the delightful little boy who first stole my heart. Hayden was only two years old when we brought Hadley home from the hospital. Like the dethroned king of the castle, he didn't appreciate this little princess getting more than her fair share of attention. Before long, however, he warmed up to his new baby sister and considered himself her utmost protector and guardian. He embraced his new role as big brother and took pride in fiercely pronouncing to visitors, "*My* baby sister!"

None of us could get enough of Hadley. Talan and I took turns letting her sleep in our arms, never taking our eyes off of her. We were enchanted by her every movement. We treasured Hadley as our most precious gift that Christmas. My husband cradling his daughter with the Christmas tree lights in the background, rocking to the soft lull of Christmas carols and the smell of wassail in the air, were Norman Rockwell moments I would never forget. Life seemed almost too good to be true. Baking, parties, and presents slowed down that year as we reveled in our new pink little package.

At that moment, I had no idea how fleeting Hadley's time as a newborn would be. As the months passed, we were shocked at how rapidly she grew. The baby clothes I had eagerly collected remained in mint condition—she wore them for only a short time before growing out of them. By the time she was six months old, Hadley could nearly pass for a toddler. Everything with Hadley was happening much too quickly.

CHAPTER THREE

April Fools

That which comes easily departs easily.
That which comes of struggle remains.

GORDON B. HINCKLEY

Just as I did with the Christmas dolls of my childhood, I carefully considered what to name my real life baby doll. "Hadley" is an English name meaning "field of heather," and it brought to my mind an image of peace and serenity befitting her sweet disposition. It was also the last name of a dear, lifelong friend. A perfect fit!

As is common in our family, Hadley soon acquired a nickname. Her older brother Hayden was nicknamed "Hay-dog," so it only seemed natural when her Uncle Bryan pronounced her "Hadcat." After she wound up in a number of unusual and dangerous predicaments, our family began to joke that Hadcat had nine lives. Hadley's series of unfortunate experiences have given her a depth of insight and perspective in her short life that many of us couldn't hope to attain, even in nine lives. Somehow, even in crisis, she always landed on her feet—and kept me on my toes!

Hadley has certainly gotten mileage out of the one life that she has been given—a life that has tested the hands of fate several times over. April 1, 1998, began as an ordinary day filled with the daily morning routines.

"Mommy, will you make Mickey Mouse pancakes, pretty please?" Hayden gave me his most convincing puppy dog face—the one that was impossible to say no to. I put away the instant oatmeal and made Hayden's favorite breakfast. Soon afterwards, I heard a soft cry coming from Hadley's room upstairs. She was a late sleeper and was now ready for her breakfast, although she would have to settle for a bottle this morning. I found her peeking over the rail of her crib, her tears now replaced by a huge grin at seeing Mommy coming to the rescue.

After Hadley and Hayden were dressed and ready for the day, I took a moment to capture a priceless picture of them sitting on our favorite birdhouse chair, with Hadley tenderly leaning on her big brother for support. Her beautiful brown, almond-shaped eyes mirrored her brother's. Hadley's wiry hair was only slightly tamed with a bow that screamed, "Yes, I *am* a girl!"

It was an unusually cold and rainy day for springtime in Arizona, making the simplest of tasks more daunting. To avoid loading and unloading the kids out of the warm car and into the rain, I decided to leave them in the car for a brief moment while I ran into the dry cleaner's. All I had to do was drop off Hadley's dress fifteen feet away from my car. In and out in thirty seconds. The thought never crossed my mind that anything bad could happen in the sleepy little town of Gilbert.

I left the car running and dashed into the cleaners, just as a young man who had been hassling the clerk was leaving. The dazed look in his dark eyes made me cringe; and while the clerk attempted to help me, I couldn't take my eyes off the disturbed young man or my car. Like a horror show playing in slow motion before my eyes, the man went straight to my car, opened the driver's door, and got in. For a split second I thought he had just confused my gold Honda Accord for his own, but it soon hit me that this was no mistake—he was trying to steal my car while my kids sat helplessly inside.

"Oh no!" I shrieked and ran frantically toward my car. The would-be carjacker didn't realize that the motor was running and kept turning the key over and over again, grinding the engine in the process but buying me precious time.

"My kids are in the car! My kids are in the car!" I screamed. I swung the door open, reached inside, and grabbed the carjacker, wrestling him out of my car. From the corner of my eye, I saw that he held something in his hand; but I thought of Hayden and Hadley, completely defenseless in the back seat, and continued to fight with him. My rage and adrenalin propelled me forward with superhuman strength. With or without a weapon, he was *not* driving away with my kids!

I managed to pull the man out of the driver's seat and into the parking lot. Then, as quickly as it began, he mumbled angrily, stumbled off, and was gone. The nightmare was over.

Tears sprang to my eyes, followed by uncontrollable weeping, as I pulled my children out of the car. I held them tightly and struggled with the unbearable "what ifs."

"Mommy, I'm scared," Hayden cried, while Hadley just looked up at me with her trusting eyes, unaware of the magnitude of what had just happened. At their tender ages, they had encountered a villain to rival those in fairy tales. I discovered that the love I had for my children was matched only by the depth of rage I felt at seeing them in danger.

Approaching sirens confirmed that the nightmare was real. The clerk at the dry cleaner's had called 911, and the police were soon speaking with me about every detail of the incident. When they left, I immediately called Talan. Incredulously, he thought I was playing an April Fool's joke on him.

"An April Fool's joke? Really!" I was livid—and reacting to the gigantic amount of adrenaline running through my system. If he had been standing there, I might have given him the same treatment that I had just given the deranged carjacker.

Once Talan realized I was serious, he dropped everything and rushed to the scene. The kids jumped into the safety of his arms, and we all basked in the love we felt as our little family was reunited. Together, we prayed with relief and expressed our deep gratitude for the protection from danger.

The rest of the day was spent at the police station and talking to reporters. I grew tired of my own voice as I had to explain every painful detail over and over again. We worked with a sketch artist to produce an eerily accurate depiction of the suspect. Hayden and Hadley were treated to stuffed animals at the police department—an oversized brown teddy bear for Hayden and a small white kitten for Hadley. With new furry friends in tow, they were both ready to return to the comfort of home.

That night, our simple routines didn't seem so simple. Each minute together was a blessing. As I wrapped up my little ones after their baths, I said another silent prayer of gratitude for their safety.

The carjacker was eventually apprehended. After attempting to steal our car, he terrorized a woman while she waited at a nearby drive-thru by repeatedly banging on her car window. He then stole an unoccupied car and drove to Tucson, Arizona, where one of his family members turned him in to the police.

I was called in to do a police line-up and identified the criminal immediately. Seeing him again sent shivers down my spine. He was sentenced to time in prison, giving us the closure we needed to put this traumatic experience behind us.

I was more careful after that ill-fated day to never take my children's safety for granted. Bad things can happen anywhere—even in our small town, even to me. Fortunately, we were spared from a devastating outcome. But happy endings, while precious, never lasted for long; there was always another challenge around the next corner. And it always seemed to involve Hadley.

Chapter Four

Humpty Dumpty

A gem cannot be polished without friction, nor a man perfected without trials.

LUCIUS ANNAEUS SENECA

After the attempted carjacking, we rode the rollercoaster of life, finding happiness in the simplest of moments. Everyone was safe, and we couldn't ask for more. But over the next few months, we grew concerned that there was something wrong with Hadley's foot. I pointed it out to my mom, and she suggested that I should have her foot checked.

Hadley was a gangly eight-month-old when she first became acquainted with her orthopedist. "What do we have here?" Dr. Milliner asked in his charming South African accent as he walked into the room. The doctor had a kind and humorous bedside manner and a natural affinity for children that put us both at ease. Hadley warmed up to him at once.

"We are worried about Hadley's right foot, because it turns inward. She is barely crawling and hasn't even attempted to stand, yet." I explained.

Dr. Milliner tickled Hadley's foot as he inspected it, which made her squeal with delight. I made a mental note to thank my friend for referring us. My friend's daughter had severe clubbed feet, which required rigorous therapy, surgeries, and corrective casts for an extended period of time.

After a few moments, Dr. Milliner gave us his diagnosis. Hadley's case was not as severe as that of my friend's daughter, but Hadley would have to wear a corrective cast covering her entire left leg for at least three months. The cast had to stay dry—something especially challenging during Arizona's hot summer months. Then, he explained, she could exchange it for a below-the-knee cast until the foot was corrected. I sighed at the news, "I guess the swimming lessons that I just signed Hadley up for will have to wait," I grumbled to myself.

Shortly thereafter, I took Hadley to the car wash. It was a busy summer afternoon, and there was a long line of cars ahead of us. After what seemed like an eternity, I saw the man drying my car wave his rag and call out, "Your car is ready!" Hadley was not yet walking, although she was getting bigger by the minute. I picked her up and carried her across the scorching asphalt.

"Come on, Sweetie. It's time to go!" I said, exhausted. In the hundred-degree heat, I felt depleted. Even Hadley had trickles of sweat running down her little face. I picked her up off the bench and took her with me to retrieve our freshly cleaned vehicle.

The intense desert heat was disorienting. The only thing I could think about was the air conditioning in our car that would soon be blowing in our faces. I was so focused on getting to my car that I tripped and went tumbling to the ground. Everything went flying—my purse, my receipt, and, worst of all, Hadley! We both landed sprawled out on the burning concrete, with Hadley taking the brunt of the fall. I carefully picked her up, worried that she had been injured.

"Hadley, Hadley, are you okay?" Hadley didn't cry and seemed to be surprisingly unscathed. So, I struggled to get my belongings together, and we moved slowly to the car, licking our wounds and desperately longing for the cool air awaiting us.

A couple of days later, I took her back to our friendly South African doctor because she was trying to crawl using only her right hand. He established that Hadley's arm had been broken in the fall and needed a cast. In disbelief I argued, "But she hasn't even been crying. Are you sure?"

The doctor explained, "Because of the nature of the break, her arm is only slightly swollen—and she must be tough as nails."

I accepted the doctor's suggestion that Hadley was unusually stoic. But I couldn't get rid of the nagging feeling that the doctor's answer was incomplete. Something didn't add up.

With a leg and an arm in casts, Hadley was beginning to remind us of Humpty Dumpty, and we worried that we would never be able to put her back together again. The doctor assured us that after all of this, she would be "as good as new."

To get out of the excruciating heat and away from the stress of daily life, especially in light of the recent debacles, I decided to take a trip with my sister to our family's mountain cabin in Pinetop, Arizona. We looked forward to a weekend filled with scrapbooking, eating, and relaxing at our home away from home.

We loaded the kids into the car and said goodbye to our husbands, who stayed behind to work.

"Be careful, and try not to have too much fun without me!" Talan said as he saw us off. My sister and I felt the temperature decrease as we approached our destination, and we grew even more excited.

A few hours later, we were surrounded by the pristine beauty of trees, flowers, and fields of grass. I breathed an audible sigh of relief. I could already feel myself relaxing as I enveloped my senses in the natural beauty that surrounded me. The kids jumped out of the car and immediately began playing outside, soaking in the cooler weather.

"Mommy, will you take us to see the horses?" Hayden pleaded.

"Okay, let me grab Hadley." I unbuckled her from the car seat, and we took the short walk to the horse corrals that were connected to our property. Hayden and his cousins spent the afternoon feeding the horses watermelon rinds and stroking their long, coarse manes, while Hadley in her casts watched intently from a shady spot on the lawn. When she grew restless, I carried her over to the corral, where the lively horses delighted her.

Everything went smoothly until the second day when Hadley began showing signs of not feeling well. Although her symptoms didn't seem to be anything more than a common cold, it bothered me that she was so out of sorts. That night I gently laid her in the crib hoping she would sleep off her sickness. But not long after I'd fallen asleep myself, she began wheezing so loud that it woke me up. When I got up to comfort Hadley, I noticed that her chest began to concave every time she tried to take a breath. It went from bad to worse very quickly.

"Oh baby, you are burning up!" I cried as I felt her forehead. Hadley was running a high temperature and was becoming extremely lethargic. My sister awoke from the commotion and became equally concerned. "What do we do?" I asked. We spent the next few minutes with a foolhardy hope that Hadley's wheezing would stop.

When Hadley's breathing became even more difficult, I anxiously called 911. "My daughter is sick!" I cried over the line in sheer panic.

The operator could hear Hadley breathing from her end of the line but urged me to remain calm. "Help is on the way," she consoled.

An ambulance arrived not long afterwards. I followed the paramedics as they carried Hadley to the ambulance only to be told that I couldn't accompany her—there was no room for me. I couldn't bear the thought of sending her alone.

"Please, is there any way I can go with her? She's only eight months old." They told me it wasn't an option, so I whispered into her ear, "Hadley, it is going to be okay. Remember Mommy loves you." I kissed her forehead, and they whisked her away.

I made the half-hour drive to the Navapache Hospital in Show Low, Arizona alone, because my sister had to stay behind with our sleeping children. That drive was one of the longest of my life. Worry consumed me as I pictured Hadley surrounded by strangers, scared and searching for my face.

She was already hooked up to a ventilator by the time I arrived at the hospital. Every breath seemed to suck the life out of her. I longed for Talan to be there—I didn't want to face this alone.

After a series of tests and x-rays, the doctors pulled me aside to give me her diagnosis—RSV.

"What does this mean? Is she going to have to stay here? Is she going to be okay?" I nervously questioned the doctors. At the time, there was not much information about this virus.

"She is a very sick little girl, and we need to keep a close eye on her," they responded soberly. With a constant prayer in my heart for Hadley's well-being, I made the emotional call to my husband.

"Jennifer," he assured, "it is going to be all right." He encouraged me to stay strong, and I knew this was something I could do, but I heard the worry in his voice. We were young parents who had never had a child in the hospital before, and we were desperately afraid of losing her. Talan made the four-hour drive to Show Low with our parents the next morning.

As hospitals go, the Navapache is about as luxurious as a Motel 6, but they took wonderful care of Hadley during her four-day visit. I slept on a flimsy, plastic mattress on the hospital floor, but I couldn't leave her side. Hadley was quite a sight. She was not only hooked up to countless machines, but she still had both her casts on. She clung to her favorite blanket for comfort—her only tangible reminder of home. The nurses couldn't believe how easy she was and began to call her their "perfect patient." During the quiet moments in the hospital, we read books and bonded without any distractions.

By the fourth day, Hadley was finally able to breathe without the aid of the ventilator. We welcomed the news that she would be released and rejoiced in the monumental turn of events.

"There is no place like home," I whispered in Hadley's ear, "and that's just where we're headed."

CHAPTER FIVE

The Nine Lives of Hadcat

A man who carries a cat by the tail learns something he can learn in no other way.

MARK TWAIN

Where is Godzilla?" asked one of our neighbors. I stopped in my tracks. I was carrying a handful of treats to the table for our neighborhood picnic at the park, where we often gathered for potluck dinners and dessert. Now that she was a gregarious toddler, Hadley loved being with her friends—they would run and play for hours. As soon as we arrived, she was off, scurrying away in her favorite red-and-white gingham dress with her little posse.

"Excuse me?" I responded, certain that I must have misunderstood my neighbor's inquiry.

She asked again, this time with a chuckle in her voice, "Where is Godzilla . . . you know, Hadley?" I could hardly believe my ears. And from an adult, no less.

"Godzilla?!" I said with disgust, summoning all my power to restrain the mother bear inside me from attacking. I walked away, stunned and speechless. With the blood boiling inside me, I sought out a bench away from everyone; this get-together had suddenly lost its allure.

As I sat alone, I heard the children giggling and screaming all around me. I heard a little voice shout, "Watch me, Mommy!" I turned in the direction of the voice and saw Hadley being pushed on a swing by her dad, enjoying herself without a care in the world.

"Hadley is going to be okay," I reminded myself. Between her frequent visits to the doctor and unusual accidents, it was a mantra that I found myself reciting often.

Overall, we loved life at our home on Loma Vista Street. We had a tight-knit group of neighbors who looked out for each other. In times of need, we exchanged meals and shared freshly baked cookies and treats regularly. We celebrated the holidays together with laughter-filled parties and decadent spreads of food. It was an idyllic neighborhood, where everyone knew one another. The streets were constantly filled with kids playing and riding bikes. It was a magical time in our lives.

As much as we loved our neighborhood parties, it was the birthday parties I planned for my kids that were the most memorable. I loved planning every detail, from the perfect theme to the coordinating plates and goodie bags. We had celebrated each of Hadley's five birthdays in this neighborhood, but her second birthday was particularly unforgettable.

The theme was butterflies, and the party included a pin-the-butterfly-on-the-flower game, a butterfly piñata, and everything else short of actual butterflies. We were ready to set up the celebration at our neighborhood park. Cake? Check. Candles? Check. Treat bags? Check. Hayden? Missing. I figured that my five-year-old must have snuck away in the pandemonium of the party preparations, so I asked Hadley where he went.

"I dunno. I think he went to a fwend's house." She murmured.

"Think really hard. Did he say what friend?" I asked, this time with more urgency. Hadley just stared at me. She had no idea where he was, and I wasn't getting anywhere with this dialogue. Panic began to set in as the start of the party was quickly approaching, and I had to find Hayden fast!

I loaded Hadley into the car and, in the frenzy, didn't bother to buckle her into the car seat; I figured we were only driving past a few houses. I scoured the street looking for Hayden. Nothing. I ran up to a couple of doors, checking friends' houses. Nothing. "Hayden, where are you?!" I yelled. I was so preoccupied with the search that I wasn't prepared for what happened next.

In absolute shock I turned around to see my car moving with Hadley in the driver's seat! Somehow, she had managed to crawl up to the front seat of our new silver Dodge Durango and pull the lever down into "Drive." She looked perfectly calm in the driver's seat, but I was anything but calm. "Hadley, stop!" I screamed.

Neighborhood kids clamored around the unfolding scene, laughing and pointing, as I raced towards Hadley and the Durango heading straight for our neighbor's house. With adrenaline-fueled speed, I reached the car without a moment to spare. I grabbed the door open, pushed Hadley aside, and slammed on the brakes. We escaped damage to the car, the house, and most importantly to Hadley. I stared at my two-year-old daughter with utter disbelief. "Hadley, what were you thinking?" I asked, incredulously.

A nonchalant "I dunno" was her only response. Another miracle. Another bullet dodged.

There was little time to recoup from this adventure, because there was now a park full of party-loving two-year-olds to host. I finally found Hayden playing in a neighbor's yard, brought him and Hadley to the park, and began the party.

Despite all of the chaos, Hadley's party was a great success. Dressed in her jean overalls with butterfly appliqués and sporting a short bob, she was the epitome of innocence. We played games, sang "Happy Birthday," and ate birthday cake. She grinned from ear to ear as she blew out the candles. I made my own private wish that Hadley would continue to be "okay." I wasn't sure how many more dangerous incidents my heart could take. I expected parenting to be tough, but those worries centered more upon potty training and getting my kids to eat green beans, not life-and-death situations. The thought of how differently the day could have gone had I not been able to stop the moving car made me shudder.

Not long after her second birthday, Hadley and I were at the shopping mall—and she was bored. Even at age two, she would much rather have played at the park or ridden her bike. We had only been to a few stores when Hadley asked if we could get a treat. Hadley loved cookies, so we headed to the Paradise Bakery on the bottom floor of the mall. As I waited in line, nibbling on samples, I suddenly realized Hadley was no longer next to me. That familiar panic set in again. I called her name louder and louder each time, but there was no response. *Where did she go?* I frantically scanned the crowd. *She couldn't have gone far. She was just standing right next to me.* How could she wander off when she was seconds from devouring a delicious cookie?

Suddenly, my eyes zeroed in on the escalator outside the bakery, where my Hadley dangled from the side as she went up towards the second floor, hanging on for dear life! I began running desperately through the crowd, hoping to reach her before she got too high. "Hadley, hold on!" I screamed.

When I was finally close enough, I jumped as high as I could, yanking her white-knuckled hands from the escalator. She fell into the safety of my arms, now shaking from the scare. My racing heart began to calm down as the few passersby that had stopped to notice us went on their way. I caught some looks of compassion and a scolding stare from a woman whose eyes said, "Keep your eye on your toddler!"

"Can we have our cookie now?" Hadley asked, already recovered and unaware of the danger.

"Of course," I sighed. Not much seemed to faze this girl. I recommitted to keeping my eyes on her and prayed I'd keep my sanity—and she'd survive—through her toddler years.

When Hadley was almost four years old, fate once again tested her nerves of steel. On occasional Saturdays, my sister and I would set up shop in an abandoned building and host a garage sale. The building sat on a busy street with plenty of traffic, which made it more likely for passersby to stop and look at our wares. I loved any excuse to de-junk—and the allure of making a little money in the process seemed like a win-win to me.

Next to shopping, one of Hadley's least favorite activities was hanging around our garage sales. For

Hadley, there was nothing fun about watching people rummage through my discarded household items.

"Not another garage sale, Mommy!" Hadley despaired.

"It will be fun. You can be Mommy's big helper." Hadley brightened when she learned that her cousin Brayden was coming along to keep her company. The two playmates pushed each other around the enormous warehouse on a dolly, dodging garage sale shoppers and filling the store with laughter.

When they got tired of pushing the dolly around the store, Hadley and Brayden discovered a wheelchair ramp that went from the front door, past the sidewalk, and directly onto the busy street. Hadley sat comfortably on the dolly with Brayden in tow, both oblivious to the looming rush-hour traffic ahead. By the time we realized what was going on, the runaway dolly was gaining momentum and couldn't be stopped. We watched the terrifying scene unfold before us in slow motion. The dolly came to a stop in the middle of the street while cars whizzed by. As if being directed by unseen hands, Hadley and Brayden navigated the oncoming traffic and got themselves back to the safety of the sidewalk.

"Oh, Hadley! You could have been killed!" I was completely beside myself. I grabbed her in a mama-bear hug and couldn't let go. The fright made my head spin.

"I am sorry, Mommy," she said with tears in her eyes. My anger instantly dissipated into relief, as I thought about what could have been. The Hadcat had, without a doubt, used up one of her nine lives that day.

The summer before Hadley was to start kindergarten, I found out that I was pregnant once again. Hadley wanted to name the baby "George" after a former pet, but I couldn't get used to the idea of naming our baby after our dead goldfish.

The baby was all Hadley could talk about. "What do you think he will look like?" "Will he look like me?" "How big will he be?" "Can I change his diaper?" The questions were never-ending. She was also my little sidekick as we got the bug-themed nursery ready, offering design critique and helpful suggestions, such as, the baby's bedroom should look just like hers.

When it seemed she could stand it no longer, Griffin finally arrived on June 21, 2001. Hadley was almost four years old at the time and delighted in her new role of big sister. Griffin didn't look like Hadley or Hayden; with his light blond hair and hazel green eyes, he had a look all his own.

Although Talan and I were now outnumbered, we relished the peaceful time spent with our three young children. Parenting is never boring, and there is a sharp learning curve. Fortunately, Hadley had survived multiple misadventures. Whenever I held my babies close, I said a silent prayer that they would continue to enjoy their childhood free from harm and that, as a parent, I would be able to meet their needs. Although Hadley was large in size, I still saw her as my baby girl. Little did we know, she would soon be forced to grow up all too quickly.

CHAPTER SIX

Pandora's Box

It is a terrible thing to see
and have no vision.

HELEN KELLER

I was raised on a street similar to Loma Vista, full of girl playmates my age. We would spend hours building elaborate sets out of cardboard, then even more time picking out the perfect costumes for our small-scale productions. We would gather our parents together for these performances, and they would shower us with applause and praise. Because I was the tallest girl, I was usually cast as the prince instead of the princess. I never argued, but it was bittersweet for me. I wanted to be a princess, too.

I received similar treatment in dance class with my same pint-sized girlfriends. I wanted to be front and center, but I always ended up on the back row. It was clear to me that I was simply tolerated by my dance teachers. I received none of the approval and praise they showered on the other dancers. They progressed quickly to more advanced classes, and I was left straggling behind. Even at my young age, I longed to be small like the other girls.

As I got older, I learned to embrace the fact that I was tall; but, I did not want that for my children. I wanted them to be *average.* When I met my future husband, I was relieved that he was only six feet tall. So, when things started unfolding with Hadley, I couldn't help but think the universe was playing a cruel joke on me.

Hadley's growth began to accelerate at an early age, which we attributed to my tall genes—but her growth was clearly beyond what I had experienced as a child. When Hadley was only three, she looked as if she could be entering kindergarten. Often when we went out to lunch, people would ask why she wasn't at school. As she entered kindergarten, she looked like a nine-year-old with baby teeth. We grew accustomed to her rapid growth spurts, and they made us more determined to enjoy every quickly passing phase.

I struggled to decide whether to start her in kindergarten at the age of four or have her wait a year. The cutoff at the public school was the end of August, but she made the December deadline at Challenger Basic School, a nearby charter school. Hadley was obviously tall for her age; but more than that, it was her curious mind and eagerness to learn that really helped us to make the decision—along with her incessant begging to join her brother and start school. She reminded me of a child taking a long road trip and asking every five minutes, "How much longer until we get there?"

Not long after she began kindergarten, Hadley had her first vision test at school. When we were notified that she had failed her eye exam, I immediately discounted it. She had shown no signs of vision problems at home, and our family generally had good eyesight. Hadley worried, but I assured her, "Honey, your eyes have never crossed, and you never sit too close to the television." I assumed that since she was young for her grade, perhaps she didn't quite understand the vision test.

I was sure it was a mistake, but I scheduled her an appointment with an optometrist just to be safe. After five minutes into her eye exam, I knew there was a problem. Of course, she struggled terribly reading the letters projected on the wall, but the biggest red flag was the troubling reaction from the doctor. After looking at her eyes through the scope, he asked if he could have one of his associates examine Hadley. I agreed, and he returned with a handful of other doctors from the office. They gathered around her as if she were a lab rat, vying to get a glimpse of whatever was at the other end of that scope.

When the other doctors finally cleared the room, our optometrist explained that Hadley had issues with the retina in one of her eyes and dislocated lenses in both. This was not uncommon in elderly patients, but it was very unusual for someone Hadley's age. He asked if Hadley had been in an accident or had received an impact that could have caused this. Hadley had been in her share of accidents, to be sure, but nothing had ever affected her eyes. We left the appointment with a referral for a specialist and the knowledge that, at the very least, Hadley would need glasses.

I didn't yet know Hadley's prognosis, but even the thought of her wearing glasses at such a young age greatly upset me. I had firsthand knowledge of how difficult vision problems could be. When I was only two and a half years old, I snuck into my neighbor's backyard, where my older brothers, Denny and Jason, were playing baseball with their friends. Despite their efforts to shoo me away, I was a stubborn little toddler and wouldn't budge. I was watching their game when a stray ball hit me directly in the middle of my right eye, lifting me off the ground.

I was inconsolable, and my brothers panicked. They called for my mom, who rushed me to our family doctor. He sent us to the emergency room, and I spent four days at the hospital lying down flat in a metal crib. The doctors hoped this would prevent further damage and allow my eye to heal. Strangely, I have vivid memories of the crib and my grandma reading to me for hours in the isolated hospital room.

Shortly after I was sent home, I walked into a door jamb and became completely disoriented. My mom realized there was still something terribly wrong with my vision and took me right back to the doctor. The specialist was eventually able to confirm my mother's greatest fear—the accident had caused my retina to detach, and I was left permanently blind in my right eye.

After the accident, I dealt not only with vision loss, but also with the unkindness that often accompanies such an impairment. "Cyclops" was just one nickname given to me by a boy in elementary school. My blindness also prevented me from doing many things, like being able to view the 3-D "Thriller" exhibit at Disneyland. Worst of all, I had a lazy eye that had a mind of its own, leaving people wondering which eye to follow. My eyes never matched up, but my parents were reluctant to have the corrective surgery performed because of the risk of losing the eye altogether. How I wished I could just be normal.

Finally, in the ninth grade, my parents relented, and I had surgery to straighten my eye. I felt less like a pariah, but the lazy eye had already wreaked havoc on my self-esteem, leaving a permanent sting that resurfaced as I now faced dealing with Hadley's vision problems—in the same eye that had plagued me in childhood.

After a month of waiting, we were able to see the retina specialist. The office was filled with gadgets and medical equipment, and Hadley's curiosity was getting the best of her. She crawled on the examination chair and fiddled with the equipment, forcing me to remember that, despite her size, she was still an active four-year-old.

The specialist confirmed there was indeed premature damage to her retina that needed to be monitored. But more concerning to him were Hadley's dislocated lenses. He inquired again whether she had suffered any kind of impact to her eyes, and I assured him she had not. This left only one other option.

"Is Hadley tall for her age?" he inquired. *Hmm . . . did he really need to ask?*

"Yes, she is extremely tall for her age," I answered.

He paused for a moment, then uttered those dreadful words that changed our lives forever: *Marfan Syndrome.*

Pandora's box had been opened. I had never heard of Marfan Syndrome before, but even the sound of it made me sick. It may as well have been Martian Syndrome!

I came home and tearfully told my husband the doctor's suspicions. At first, Talan took the news in stride, encouraging me to be positive. We'd had plenty of scares in the past and everything had always turned out fine. But once we began scouring the Internet, we became more and more worried as each new symptom seemed to fit Hadley's challenges—such as her large stature and her newly found vision problems. But the symptoms we could not see were even more alarming.

Marfan Syndrome, we quickly learned, is a genetic disorder of the connective tissues. It creates weak ligaments, which affect the functioning of all parts of the body—especially the heart, the eyes, the back, and the skin. We saw photos of men, women, and children with Marfan Syndrome and cringed at the possibility that our Hadley was suffering from the disease.

Our next medical appointment was with a geneticist who confirmed after many extensive tests that Hadley did, in fact, have Marfan Syndrome. We were sent to a long list of doctors: pediatric cardiologists, orthopedists, endocrinologists, and ophthalmologists. We even traveled to the City of Hope in California to meet with a special team of doctors who work exclusively with Marfan Syndrome patients. While we were there, Hadley underwent more extensive genetic testing, and we discovered that her case was caused by a random genetic mutation. This bittersweet diagnosis meant that we didn't need to worry about her siblings carrying this gene—it was uniquely hers.

My heart ached as I tried to process all we had just learned. When you receive a diagnosis like this, your whole world changes instantly. The visions and dreams you have for your child are drastically altered, and you mourn the life you envisioned for your child.

Imagining the obstacles your child will surely face can be overwhelming and leave you feeling helpless. The depth of anguish and despair is indescribable. Through many sleepless, tear-filled nights, I struggled helplessly to find peace. I often thought of what my Grandma Barney always said: "The best way to eat an elephant is one bite at a time." Marfan Syndrome was now that elephant.

That peace would come and go, many times because of the well-meaning but misdirected attempts to console me. After one particularly long and strenuous eye appointment with her ornery ophthalmologist—who complained incessantly that seeing Hadley was like seeing three patients in one because of her extensive problems (he even doubled my co-pay!)—my emotions got the best of me. The ophthalmologist responded by chastening me that I should be grateful, because so many children have it worse than my daughter. His lack of compassion stunned me. The fact that other children experienced more severe problems didn't make it any easier for Hadley.

I never appreciated when people began a sentence with, "At least . . ." Even friends were quick to point out that "at least" it wasn't this, or "at least" it wasn't that. Coming from people who had perfectly healthy children, it did little to comfort me. I did struggle with guilt, thinking that others were suffering more than we were, but sometimes hearing that from others came across as condescending and insensitive rather than helpful. Yes, it could be worse—but what we were living through was bad enough, and it was all I could do to accept our new reality and try to make the best of it.

In Hadley's case, there were many unknowns. We knew she had an enlarged aorta along with a prolapsed mitral valve, but we didn't know how critical her heart condition was. The biggest concern with the heart is that over time, the weak connective tissue can cause the aorta to stretch and dilate, putting the aorta at risk of a sudden tear. This life-threatening condition, called "dissection," may cause blood to leak out if not properly treated. Hadley was prescribed beta blockers right away to help her heart pump more easily, which lessened the deterioration of the blood vessels. It was the risk of dissection that prohibited Hadley from playing contact sports, especially basketball.

The condition of Hadley's eyes was initially the most pressing issue. We had known for some time that she had severe vision problems. Hadley was nearsighted in one eye, farsighted in the other, and suffered from astigmatism. She had become accustomed to seeing with double vision. The lens in Hadley's right eye had to be removed, because the ligaments were so weak that the lens was always shifting, making it impossible to see. It was as if she were wearing a contact lens that covered only half of her eye. It had to be removed, not replaced, because a new lens would follow the same pattern due to the weak ligaments.

By Hadley's third surgery, a cataract removal, she pleaded, "Mom, do I really have to do this again?" I hated to see her go through another eye surgery, but of course the answer was "yes." Fortunately, Hadley's left eye was not yet as severely damaged as her right eye; but, it was likely that her left eye would eventually need the same operation. Without the aid of contacts and glasses, she was nearly blind.

Hadley came home from each of these operations in terrible pain, with gauze patches covering her eyes. Her eyes itched terribly, but she couldn't touch them due to the risk of infection. There wasn't much she could do during these times, but she loved to be read to and even have her toenails and fingernails painted (something she didn't usually like). The silver lining during these difficult days was the quiet time we were able to spend together.

Hadley also suffered from severe scoliosis, but her weak ligaments made it untreatable. She was extremely flexible and limber. One of the more troubling concerns with Marfan Syndrome is that some women are unable to have children—and, if they do, their children have a 50% chance of having the condition, as well. If not monitored properly, Marfan Syndrome can result in death. Fortunately, we were reassured by the fact that Hadley was diagnosed at a young age. This enabled us to take preventive measures and monitor her closely.

Besides heart, vision, back, and ligament problems, Hadley was faced with a very obvious symptom of her disease: excessive height. How tall would Hadley be? At the suggestion of the doctor, we attempted to stall Hadley's growth with the help of an experimental hormone therapy. The drawback was that she started having her monthly cycle at the early age of nine. There were no guarantees that the hormones would work, but we felt an urgency to try. In the end, the results were not what we had hoped for. Hadley grew well past the projected height of 5'11".

The first time we met with her endocrinologist—one whose obsession with all things Snoopy had overtaken every nook and cranny of her office—she asked Hadley to draw a picture of herself. Hadley took her time, and the finished drawing was remarkable. Hadley drew herself surrounded by flowers, trees, grass, and birds, with the sun shining down upon them like a benevolent parent. It was cheerful and bright, just like Hadley. But what caught our attention most of all was the huge smile on Hadley's face as she stood next to a house. In the drawing, the rooftop of the house and the top of her head met at the same place in the crayon-blue sky. The endocrinologist and I marveled that Hadley acknowledged her height and accepted it so readily. But behind the smile, Hadley was having a difficult time, as she states in her own words below.

On a Friday afternoon in February 2002, my life changed forever. My kindergarten class had its yearly health exam, where they checked your hearing, sight, and if you had any lice. The first test I took was to check my hearing, and I aced it. The next one was the sight test. They started with the letter chart. They told me to read off the fourth row first, and I couldn't see a single letter. So, they pointed at the third row, and I couldn't see that one, either. After they checked the second row (and I bombed that one too), they called my mom and told her I had failed my sight test. I didn't think anything was wrong with my vision, because I didn't think anyone could see the board from the first row in the classroom. I had to always go up to the board, because I couldn't see from my seat. It could have been worse. Luckily, I didn't fail the lice test.

When my mom heard that news, she wasn't very worried. She figured it was just a silly little school test, but just to be safe, she made an appointment for me at the eye doctor's office. When I went to the doctor, I was a little nervous. I never liked going to the doctor. We got there, and my mom signed me in. We had to wait in the waiting room for about an hour before they finally called me back.

The first thing they did was do the test where I guessed the letters on the screen. It turns out the test at school wasn't a fraud, because in both eyes I was seeing 80/20. After the test, they dilated my eyes. They saw that my lens was dislocated in my eye. If you don't know what an eye lens is, it's basically what makes your eye see clearly.

I was then sent to see an eye specialist. After he did a series of tests on my eyes, he said, "Does your daughter have any heart condition or back issues?"

My mom quickly responded, saying, "No, why?"

The doctor went on to tell her that I might have a genetic disorder called Marfan Syndrome. He thought this was what caused my awful vision. Marfan Syndrome is a genetic disorder that causes your ligaments to be weak, which was causing the dislocation of my right lens.

Marfan Syndrome affects other parts of your body, such as your back, height, and heart. They sent me to a genetic doctor just to make sure, and the tests confirmed that I did have Marfan Syndrome. I had to go to all of the doctors just to figure out more and more stuff that was wrong with me. I had back issues, but they couldn't do anything about it. Whatever they did to fix my weak ligaments would just shift my spine right back.

I started going to the doctor about once a month and getting surgeries on my eyes. Each time we would get so frustrated, because nothing was changing and nothing was getting better. I even had to get my right lens removed, so now I am almost blind in that eye. Everything is just a complete blur.

The worst news of all was that I could no longer play basketball because of my heart issues. My aorta was already too big, and they didn't want it to expand and possibly blow up, which could hurt me. I was devastated, because all I ever wanted to do was play basketball. I was positive that was what I was destined to do. Ever since I was in preschool, my dream was to play in the WNBA. That's all I ever talked about—that's all I ever dreamed about. I couldn't imagine that doing something I loved could kill me; it was such a terrible feeling. I didn't have a dream, anymore. I could no longer do what I wanted to do. I think that's what hurt my mom and me the most. I felt like all my height just went to waste. It just got thrown down the garbage disposal. In just one instant, my dreams were demolished.

While Hadley experienced depths of grief often unknown to girls her age, she was astonishingly resilient. "Rubber Band Disease," the slang term for Marfan Syndrome, was fitting for Hadley, who rebounded quickly. Bouncing back was not always easy for me, however. At times I felt hopeless, deflated, and defeated. What I didn't know was that Marfan Syndrome, the very disease that threatened to take her life, would actually save it.

Beach beauty, July 1998

Hadley at four years old, December 2001

A painting of Hadley and her girlfriends for a children's book, 2003

Hadley and Hayden the morning of the carjacking, April 1998

THE
Tribune
SERVING THE COMMUNITIES OF THE EAST VALLEY
VOL. 50, NO. 87 THURSDAY APRIL 2, 1998

Mother fights off carjacker in Gilbert

2 children were in car when man jumped in

BY BILL DAVIS
THE TRIBUNE

MOTHER: Fights off carjacker

From Page **A1**

store entrance 10 feet away when a young man with a buzz haircut and wearing a baggy sweat shirt, jeans and hiking boots rushed past her and jumped into the driver's seat.

Nielson doesn't remember how long she stood in stunned disbelief as the man kept turning the ignition key in the running car. "I remember thinking 'What

Mesa Tribune *newspaper article, April 1998*

Little Miss Humpty Dumpty,
July 1998

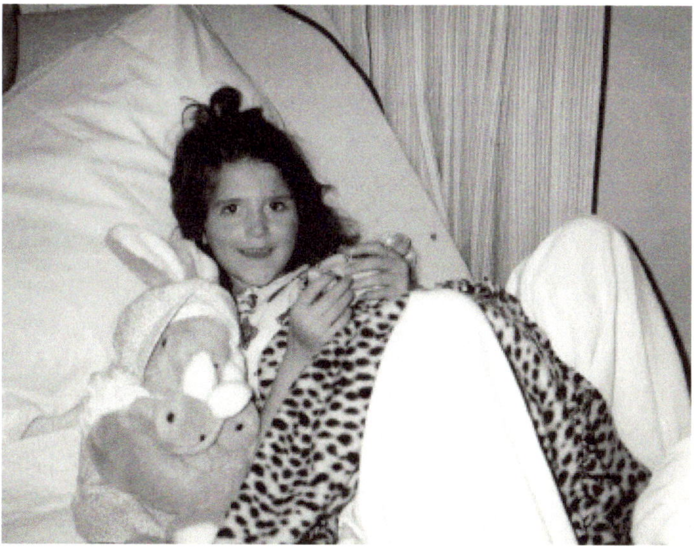

Hadley at the hospital after she was run over, February 2003

Hadley's depiction of herself "as big as a house," April 2003

Even in first grade, Hadley loved being tall, December 2004

Delivering treats to the orphanage in Mexico, October 2006

"Hadley's Vision" Fundraiser Ad Picture, May 2006

Hadley receiving the Golden Rule Award, February 2007

Hadley and Grandpa Barney at the ranch, August 1999

The last picture with Grandpa Barney at the ranch, August 2008

Hadley in her Elite Club basketball jersey, March 2012

Hadley playing basketball, March 2012

Annual Family Christmas Card picture, November 2011

Hadley, fourteen years old, November 2011

Chapter Seven

Valentine's Day

There is no charm equal to
tenderness of heart.

JANE AUSTEN

During her kindergarten year, Hadley and I had a special arrangement. Once a week I would take her on a date during the second half of school. The first half of the day was mostly academic, but the second was filled with art and other activities that were more hands-on and less structured. It made the transition a little easier, since we both loved spending time together and Hadley was still so young. This became a highly anticipated day for both of us throughout kindergarten. One of our dates fell on February 14. She picked out a special, brand-new outfit to wear to her class's Valentine's Day party and over to her grandma's in the afternoon.

I was still trying to make sense of the diagnosis we had just received. It had only been a week since we had met with the geneticist, and it was a lot to take in. My heart was still tender with thoughts of Hadley and how her life would be forever changed. As I watched her take part in her class party, exchanging Valentine's Day cards and treats with her classmates, the irony of the situation was almost too much to bear. The perfectly shaped hearts on the cards Hadley exchanged with her classmates seemed a cruel contrast in my mind with the imperfect heart beating inside of her. I winced.

"Happy Valentine's Day, Mom," Hadley said as she handed me a beautiful handmade card. On the front was a picture of us standing next to each other holding hands and surrounded by flowers, with the sun shining brightly in the sky. Little hearts decorated the front of the card. Inside she had written, *"Roses are red, violets are blue, I wish I were as beautiful as you."* Tears sprang to my eyes. It occurred to me that I should be the one comforting her instead of the other way around. That priceless card remains a treasure that is still stored safely in her memory box.

By the time the Valentine's party had ended, it was way past Griffin's naptime, and he was exhausted. We drove to my mom's house, and I carried him to a crib she kept for her grandkids. Hadley was distracted by her favorite red Radio Flyer tricycle sitting in the garage and asked if she could ride it in the driveway. "Okay, I will be out there in just a minute," I said. She made her way to the driveway and rode around in circles, off in her own little world. Her long legs stuck out on each side of the steering wheel, but she didn't seem to mind that she had almost outgrown the tricycle. It was a rainy, overcast day, but this didn't hamper Hadley's spirit as she enjoyed this moment of pure delight. That moment of childhood bliss was shattered when my sister pulled in the driveway. They had waved at each other, but somehow Hadley ended up in the wrong place at the wrong time—and somehow, inconceivably, Hadley was run over by my sister's Suburban.

Suddenly, I heard terrible screams coming from outside—enough to know something was terribly wrong. When my sister and my mom came through the back door carrying Hadley, it was worse than I could have imagined. Hadley had passed out on impact and was unconscious. How I would have welcomed tears! Her head was bleeding profusely, and it was already beginning to swell. We laid her on the kitchen floor, still semi-conscious, as I desperately called 911. Weeping and wailing filled the room. It was a horrific scene.

The operator wanted me to stay on the phone, but I couldn't stand up any longer. The world was spinning around me. My knees were weak, and I was so close to fainting that I had to kneel down. On my knees I began praying desperately, begging and pleading for a miracle. I bartered that I would do anything in return if she would just be spared. I would have traded places with her if I could have. The thought of losing her was overwhelming.

At last the paramedics arrived. They removed the remains of Hadley's clothes, which revealed large tire tracks across her stomach, and got to work on her immediately. I couldn't control my sobbing as I watched them working to save my sweet girl. The plan was to take her by ambulance to the church parking lot behind my parents' house so the air evac would have a place to land. From there she would be flown to the Maricopa County Hospital in Phoenix. I did not want Hadley to go alone this time. The paramedics told me that there was room for one person but that I could only come if I could compose myself. I said another silent prayer and found the strength to pull it together. Hadley needed her mom to be strong more than anything else at that moment, and I was not going to let her down.

Hadley was strapped to a stiff board with a brace around her neck. She was covered in blood that wouldn't stop flowing. It was raining outside, and I could see Hadley licking the raindrops on her lips. It was the first promising sign of life.

Hadley became coherent enough that she protested getting in the helicopter, and not until after the accident did I understand why. Hadley later recounted a dream she'd had prior to the accident—more of a nightmare, really—in which she was forced to go on a helicopter ride while she was strapped to a board with blood all around her, while "evil" men in black tried to take her away against her will. Naturally, that explained her fear and apprehension. Nevertheless, the helicopter transport went smoothly and gave me a few short moments alone with her. "Hadley, how are you feeling?" I was finally able to ask.

She whispered, "I hurt all over. Mommy, I'm scared. It even hurts to cry."

I did my best to comfort her. "Honey, you just keep being brave. Those doctors are going to take good care of you!" As we were landing at the hospital, I could see Talan getting out of my dad's red SUV. He had been eating lunch at a nearby restaurant with my dad and brothers when they got the call about Hadley's accident. Amazingly, we all arrived together.

Hadley looked horrendous as she was rushed out of the air evac into the hospital. There was just enough time for Talan to see her and to kiss her forehead, although he nearly collapsed at seeing his precious daughter looking the way she did. "How is my little girl?" he asked, but she was rushed along before she could answer him.

A team of doctors moved into action to help Hadley, but for us, time was standing still. We prayed desperately but knew it was out of our hands. We didn't know what kind of internal injuries Hadley had suffered or how severe they might be. It was a torturous waiting game now. We paced the hospital floor for what seemed like an eternity.

When the doctors finally came out of the operating room, we anxiously huddled, awaiting their report. It was the moment we had all been waiting for, but were we prepared for what they would report? The doctor looked at the large crowd of family and friends huddled together and then spoke gently. "Hadley has a brain concussion. We've done a complete evaluation of her other major organs, and other than some bumps and bruises, she has not suffered any extensive injuries. To tell you the truth, it is unbelievable, considering the impact she sustained. I believe that because of Marfan's, her ligaments and organs were able to stretch like elastic—and that probably saved her life. She is a lucky little girl." I knew it wasn't just luck. Our hearts were full as we shed tears of joy and offered silent prayers of gratitude.

We were stunned. Relief and tears of joy flooded the room. Even the nurses were moved by the wonderful news.

When we were finally able to visit Hadley in the recovery room, Talan, through teary eyes, made promises of a new puppy and a trip to Disneyland. It brought a small smile to her face. Her head was still swollen, and her hair was caked with blood. Our tall girl looked small once again in the full-sized hospital bed. The doctors needed to keep Hadley overnight at the hospital for observation. We were crowded into a room with three other families for this hospital sleepover—a night that rivaled our stay at the Navapache Hospital. Although the night was filled with commotion, crying babies, and very little sleep, I felt nothing but overwhelming joy that Hadley was going to be okay.

The next morning, as she was playing with her new Barbies, Hadley called for me. "Mommy, I am feeling sick," she said softly. As she tried to get up she turned a gray-green color and then suddenly passed out cold. The nurses frantically ran to her aid and managed to revive her quickly. Upon further examination her doctor determined she just needed to take it slow and urged us to watch her closely. "But," he continued, "She's going to be fine." Hadley had dodged the biggest bullet of all this time.

It was hard to believe that just one week before, we had received the difficult news that Hadley had Marfan Syndrome. Not long before that, I was agonizing over the fact that she would have to wear glasses. That no longer seemed like such a burden. Our close call with Hadley put everything into perspective. This excruciating experience turned out to be a gift, because it helped to soften the pain of her diagnosis. Hadley was still with us, and that was enough. Our glass was half full again! Her "Rubber Band Disease" had saved her life, and I was suddenly grateful for it. It was the best Valentine's Day gift I could ever have received.

It was a Friday afternoon at school and, as usual, my mom picked me up early for lunch. As I sat in the car, I got the usual lecture from her about how important school was. She wanted me to work hard so I could get smart.

"Hadley, are you sure you want to leave on Valentine's Day?" my mom tried to persuade me. She said, "I think it would be good if you just stayed here. You might miss out on something fun and maybe learning something too." I told my mom, "I'm only in kindergarten. It's not a big deal, Geez." Like always, I won! She took me to Grandma Barney's house.

When we got to my grandma's house, I told my mom, "I'm so bored." All she said back was, "Hadley, we just pulled up to the driveway. We haven't even gotten out of the car yet!" When I got out of the automobile I went straight for the tricycle. Man, that was a blast! I always loved riding my tricycle.

While I was enjoying myself, I looked up and thought, "Oh goody, there's my aunt coming up the street." I drove down the driveway to say hi to my aunt DD. When I was by the window, I said, "Hi, whatup Aunt D. What's happenin'?" Then I turned around and drove back up the driveway.

When I was getting ready to go inside, I wasn't paying attention. I went to park my tricycle in the spot where my aunt would sometimes park. While I was sitting there day dreaming, my aunt was pulling into the parking spot. When I saw that she didn't see me, I mumbled to myself, "What is she doing? She should be slowing down by now!" At this point, I was freaking out. I realized, "Oh my gosh, she doesn't see me!"

Suddenly, I was knocked off my tricycle, and my head was slammed against the ground. I thought it was over, but she was still moving forward. That's when my life flashed before my eyes. I thought this was it, my life was over!

Then I felt an excruciating pain in my stomach. She ran over me! I really just got run over! *I panicked. I thought I was dead. I was numb throughout my entire body. After a couple of seconds I heard something, and relief washed over me, because that noise was me crying.*

My aunt didn't know what just happened. She must have felt like she had run over a speed bump (but the last time I checked there were no speed bumps on the driveway). Then she heard me crying. Right at that moment she realized what just happened. She had run over her five-year-old niece! "Ah, ah, oh my gosh, oh my gosh!" I heard my aunt scream hysterically.

I felt like I was lying there for centuries when I heard the loudest scream of my life! My grandma had run out the back door and seen her granddaughter lying on the concrete. Then I passed out. They both scooped me into their arms not knowing if I were still alive. They carried me into the house, and it was then that my mom saw her mangled daughter. She began crying hysterically too, and then she frantically called 911! She feared if they didn't come soon, I could die!

When the paramedics finally arrived, I was sent by air evac to the hospital. When I came to again, I was relieved to see my mom at my side and that she was going to come with me on the helicopter. I didn't want to go alone!

The ride in the helicopter wasn't as scary as I thought it would be. It took a long time at the hospital for them to figure out if I was okay! Every time I would move, the machine on my arm would beep. I couldn't wait to get it off. When they finally told me that everything was going be fine, I was on cloud nine! I still hurt all over, but I didn't care. All I wanted to do now was to see my mom and dad! They couldn't stop hugging me when they came in my room. I was just as happy to see them as they were to see me. I couldn't stop smiling as I thought about how lucky I was to still be alive!

CHAPTER EIGHT

Honest Abe

Be who you are and say what you feel,
because those who mind don't matter,
and those who matter don't mind.

DR. SEUSS

There was once a man who found a butterfly cocoon. He picked it up carefully, placed it in his jacket, and brought it home to watch the transformation from cocoon to butterfly. A few weeks passed. One bright morning, the butterfly began to work its way out of the cocoon. It struggled for several hours to force its body through the small hole that had appeared. It stopped making progress and seemed to be stuck, so the man in his kindness decided to help the butterfly. He took a pair of scissors and snipped off a bit of the cocoon. The butterfly soon emerged with ease, but it had a swollen body and small, shriveled wings. The butterfly never learned to fly. The struggle to work its way out of the cocoon was what the butterfly needed to help its wings grow and gain the strength to fly. Freedom and flight came only after the struggle.

Allowing our children to struggle and learn on their own is often excruciating to watch—and it goes against every impulse we have to protect our children. But as hard as it was, Talan and I resisted the urge to intervene and protect Hadley from unpleasant circumstances; as a result, we watched Hadley emerge from the cocoon of disability due to Marfan Syndrome and grow physically, socially, and spiritually.

As parents just learning to deal with Marfan's and coming to terms with Hadley's limitations, we were determined to do whatever it took to provide her with a positive environment and normal daily life. Fortunately, at Challenger Basic School the culture of tolerance and opportunity allowed Hadley to blossom and grow without discrimination from those around her. By the time Hadley was in fifth grade she had outgrown everyone at her school! She was not only the tallest student at her school, but she also towered over the principal and all the teachers. Her height meant she had to stand on the floor during school productions instead of the bleachers with her fellow classmates. At the age of eleven, she was 5'11" and wore size 11 shoes. Even with her unique circumstances, this school provided her with a perfect platform to nurture and express her individuality.

The "back to the basics" school philosophy focused on cultivating an environment of respect and moral development. Hadley once informed me, "Mom, Hayden said the 'S' word." This caught me by surprise—but when he admitted his guilt, it turned out the bad word he had said was "shut up," not the other "S" word. I appreciated the high standards upheld by the school and it was a blessing to Hadley. She was insulated from the roughness and cruelty that I knew she would be exposed to on the playgrounds of public schools. Instead of mistreatment, Hadley was known and loved at her school. It was this environment that prompted Hadley to write in an essay, *"I don't feel like I'm different from all the other kids because of Marfan Syndrome. Everyone has problems in life. Nobody is perfect."*

Not everything about school has been easy, however. Hadley has always stood out from other kids in the school because of her condition. Not only has she always been extremely tall, but many of her features and extremities are long, including her spider-like fingers (a condition called "arachnodactlyly"). The kids noticed her differences, so Hadley responded by doing tricks with her long, flexible limbs. Her favorite is twisting her thumbs upside down on the back of her hands.

The only drawback to this remarkable school was the long drive—it took about twenty-five minutes to get there. Getting out the door in the morning was always a little crazy, and it was not uncommon for lunches, homework, and even articles of clothing to be left behind. One morning in particular, Hayden bellowed from the back of the car, "Mom, I forgot my shoes." Of course he failed to point this out until we were pulling up to the school.

"Hayden, how do you forget shoes? I am not driving all the way back home!" We would have been almost an hour late to school. His helpful, albeit mischievous, little sister offered, "Hayden, you can borrow my shoes!" and she handed him her blue and pink flip flops that happened to have been left in the car. Much to his dismay and her delight, Hayden wore his sister's shoes to school that day.

Some medical experts suggest that Marfan Syndrome causes learning disabilities. Although we were prepared for this possibility, Hadley has always done well academically, only needing occasionally to be redirected. And while humor is a wonderful coping mechanism

Hadley uses to cope with her condition, it sometimes gets in the way of her learning. While Hadley is different from other children in some ways, for the most part she has blended in the ways that matter most.

Due to the small size of the school, Hadley and Hayden were in a combined fifth and sixth grade class one year. Hayden was resistant, but I insisted we give it a try. Hadley, on the other hand, was elated to be in the same class as her big brother. Fortunately, it turned out to be a positive experience for both of them. Talan and I loved to meet at the school often for a lunch date with Hayden and Hadley. We would have our own little picnic under the shade of the trees, and the kids would quickly devour their food, anxious for what usually came next—basketball. Hadley especially couldn't wait to get out to the playground with her dad and brother to fill the rest of their time at recess with this much-anticipated game. There was always a large group of kids who excitedly joined in.

In that fifth grade classroom, Hadley discovered an unexpected connection with Abraham Lincoln. It has been suggested that he too had Marfan Syndrome. He displayed many of the physical characteristics associated with this condition, such as height, long face, flexible/loose joints, droopy eyelids, sunken chest, arched palate, and saggy skin. (Other than her height and stretch marks, Hadley does not have many of the more severe physical characteristics that often accompany Marfan's.) Hadley learned that Abraham Lincoln also had three sons that died before the age of twenty, and his mother died at the early age of thirty-four—all deaths that were possibly brought on by the effects of Marfan Syndrome.

Besides her height, Hadley holds another characteristic in common with Abraham Lincoln: honesty. Hadley is 100% honest and was even honored with the Honesty Award in fifth grade. One Christmas Hadley informed me I was going to love the gift Dad was giving me. "It is soooo big you can sit in it!" she gleefully informed me. Hmm. Needless to say, the Suburban sitting in my driveway Christmas morning didn't come as a huge surprise. Hadley simply cannot tell a lie, even when it might benefit her. When I came home to muddy footprints from the front door to the laundry room, Hadley immediately confessed, "Mom, it is all my fault. I begged Hayden to go play out in the mud with me. But it was so much fun!" She knew she was in for it but still didn't try to hide her guilt. She is our little "Honest Abe."

Hadley had loved watching her brother Hayden portray Abraham Lincoln in their school program, so when the opportunity presented itself for Hadley to do the same the following year, she immediately raised her hand. "I will do it!" she announced. It was an unusual choice for a girl to portray Abraham Lincoln, but Hadley was elated. She immediately came home and began soliciting her brother's help in assembling her costume—a suit of Hayden's, a tall black hat, and a makeshift beard. On the day of the program, Hadley stood tall and proud as she represented this honorable man. Even her Grandma Barney, who was a little apprehensive that this might negatively impact her self-esteem, quickly changed her mind when she saw the satisfaction on Hadley's face.

After much deliberation, Hadley left Challenger Basic School during the middle of her sixth grade year. We had just moved into a new home that was within bike riding distance to an elementary school. For me, it was thrilling to send my children off to school, waving them goodbye from the front doorstep instead of making that tedious drive every day. It also gave Hadley an opportunity to meet the kids who would be her junior high peers. Hadley made friends easily and was finding her place in her new world, although she learned quickly that all children weren't as nice as those at her old school. When Hadley observed one particularly intolerant girl bullying another girl, she stepped in to defend the victim, putting herself directly in the bully's line of fire. The bully immediately scorned, "It's none of your business. Besides, you're a giant, and nobody likes you, anyway." When Hadley came home from school, she replayed the events of the day, only casually mentioning this incident without seeming overly affected by it.

"So, how did you respond?" I asked.

Hadley answered, "I just ignored her. I don't think she's very happy anyway because, you know, I'm the new girl, and she's jealous because I am getting all the attention." Hadley didn't waste her time wondering if there was any validity to the girl's unkind remarks; she simply moved on, understanding that the other girl's unhappiness was not her problem. Even when Hadley was younger, she articulated this philosophy: "You should have a loving heart no matter what someone does to you. You have to learn to forgive, even when it's hard."

I often remind my kids: "It is better to do the right thing than impress the wrong people." Hadley lives that principle better than anyone I know.

Hadley is blessed with an especially keen sense of humor that draws others to her. One particularly crazy morning in second grade, Hadley showed up at school wearing her shirt inside out. After a friend pointed this out to her, Hadley quickly countered, "It's the latest style!" then made a mad dash to the bathroom to fix her shirt. A few minutes later, the same friend approached Hadley with her shirt on inside out, only to find Hadley had changed back. Confused, her friend asked Hadley, "Why did you change your shirt?"

Hadley retorted, "Inside out was so five minutes ago!"

Hadley was blessed with thick skin and a great sense of humor, but an even more important attribute is her kindness towards others. Mothers often approach me expressing gratitude for Hadley's friendship to their daughters. "If it weren't for Hadley, I would have a difficult time getting my daughter to school," one mom told me in confidence. Often, these are girls who feel they have no other friends. Hadley has an internal radar for those who need a friend or a little extra kindness; and lifting their spirits is a gift that comes as naturally to her as breathing.

Chapter Nine

Hadley's Vision

One person can make a difference.

JOHN F. KENNEDY

When I was growing up, my father impressed upon me the Golden Rule, "Do unto others as you would have others do unto you." That was his answer for every problem in my life—whether tattling on a sibling for being mean or dealing with unkind friends at school. At times I would get frustrated and want different advice. I didn't always want to "do unto others" as I would want them to do; sometimes I wanted to retaliate and return the unkindness.

My dad was part of the Arizona Interfaith Council, an organization that unites all different religions under the umbrella of "the golden rule." Every year the organization hosts a charity banquet honoring people in the community that live that rule through service in the community. When Hadley was eight, she was my date to this function because her dad wasn't able to attend. Hadley was so inspired by this evening and the stories she heard of others' service that we spent the half-hour drive home brainstorming different ideas of how we could make a difference. This is when "Hadley's Vision" was born.

In the summer of 2005, just after we had our fourth child, Lincoln, our family began taking regular trips down to The Mayan Palace in Rocky Point,

Mexico. We would stay at a beautiful resort where the kids loved playing on the beach, painting ceramics, and swimming in the pool. We looked forward to afternoon bingo games and virgin Piña Coladas at happy hour. All we had was time. And I wanted time to enjoy my new little baby. Lincoln was another blond-haired baby boy with big blue eyes that set him apart from the rest of his siblings.

While on a trip to Rocky Point in the fall, we noticed a little dirt road off the highway with a sign that read, "Orphandad." We were intrigued and made the long drive down the dusty road to discover an orphanage right there in the middle of nowhere. The man in charge welcomed our family in, and we immediately fell in love with these children who greeted us with enthusiasm and wonder. They proudly showed us their rooms, where they each had their own bunk bed. There was a big rec hall where the thirty or so children gathered for meals and entertainment. Everything was in perfect order and very tidy. The area that seemed to get the most use was the dusty courtyard that served as a refuge for the children. They would run and climb all over the playground set. It was a happy place, miraculously void of the feeling of abandonment you might expect at an orphanage.

The next time we visited, we decided to bring a treat for each of these endearing children. We created special packages with a bag of Skittles, a notebook, crayons, and bubbles. They were so overjoyed with this small act of kindness that we resolved to provide Christmas for the orphanage. We received a detailed list of the children's names and ages from the director so we could find an outfit and a toy that would perfectly suit each of them. We made this happen for these deserving children with the help of my entire family.

The Christmas season was upon us, and we were busy with our holiday preparations. It was only two weeks away when we took the much-anticipated trip to the orphanage to deliver the presents. In tow was our new family dog, Lilly—the fulfillment of an earlier promise to Hadley. Our kids will attest that it was one of our best Christmases ever! The joy and appreciation that each of these sweet children expressed was as much of a gift to us as our packages were to them. We stayed for hours watching the children as they played with their new toys. It was a happy moment where we all felt what Christmas is really about. This opportunity to serve created a desire in Hadley to do even more.

Hadley decided to put on a carnival to raise funds for needy children with vision problems. The first step was raising donations and collecting items for the silent auction. Hadley knew just what to say as she went from business to business talking confidently with adults about her fundraiser. Hadley was barely eight at the time and people were captivated with this unexpectedly poised young girl and responded generously with donations. It was quite impossible to say "no" to Hadley.

Our whole family became involved with organizing the carnival. It was a huge undertaking! We worked together mailing out invitations and calling people, and Hadley was involved in every step. Balloons lined the perimeter of my parents' backyard, and banners hung with the words, "Hadley's Vision." We had pony rides, multiple bouncers, a dunking machine, a professional balloon artist, face painting, cotton candy, popcorn, snow cones, pizza, a cake walk, and several other booths and prizes. Hadley's favorite part of the night was getting dunked over and over in the dunking machine—a reminder of this joyful child's amazing spirit.

The generous donations of friends, families, and members of the community made this event possible. No admission was charged; people just donated an amount of their choice. The turnout and generosity of others exceeded our expectations. The Hadley's Vision carnival raised over eight thousand dollars that evening—an overwhelming success! The next day, Hadley personally delivered thank you notes and cookies to all those who contributed time and/or money toward this cause.

After this event, Hadley was interviewed by a local newspaper about Hadley's Vision and how it came about. The interviewer took my eight-year-old aside and asked what motivated her to take on this huge endeavor. Hadley responded, "It felt really good because my mom was not pushing me to do it. I had the choice of whether or not I should do it. I just wanted all kids to have the help and support that I have had." That's what Hadley's Vision was all about.

The crowning moment of this experience came the following year at the Arizona Interfaith charity dinner, where Hadley was honored with the "Golden Rule" award for her efforts to "do unto others as you would have others do unto you." Hadley became the youngest recipient of this award and was again highlighted on the evening news, proudly receiving this award with thousands of people looking on. There was hardly a dry eye as she was given a standing ovation from the entire audience. What a memorable evening! Hadley's award is still displayed in our home as a reminder of this cherished honor that was bestowed upon her for thinking of others before herself.

Part of the money raised from Hadley's Vision was donated to Southwestern Eye Center for the humanitarian work it does in Mexico. As a result, we traveled to Colonial Dublan to take part in and see the benefits of the donation first-hand. We loaded the bus at 5:00 A.M. on a September morning for a seven-hour trip down to Dublan. The time was filled with inspiring stories from participants who had gone in previous years. Ten-year-old Hayden, eight-year-old Hadley, and four-year-old Griffin were by far the youngest on the trip (Lincoln stayed home with his Grandma Nielson), but they were on their best behavior and willingly contributed to this humanitarian effort.

The welcome we received in Dublan from the people in the community was truly heartwarming. We were treated like royalty. We were provided with a comfortable hotel room that was within walking distance from the town hospital. The hotel was modeled after a traditional hacienda with white stucco and a red tile roof. The courtyard of the hotel was covered in green grass and had a large fountain sitting in the center. We felt right at home.

Hadley was able to observe countless cataract surgeries to correct dislocated lenses performed on individuals that would have otherwise had to live with their vision problems. Starting at sunrise, a line formed around the building as talented doctors worked tirelessly, performing surgery after surgery. The patients left with patches over their eyes knowing that, in time, their vision and their lives would never be the same.

One young man who came through the line had Marfan Syndrome. He was in his mid-twenties and suffered from cataracts. He did not have access to the opportunities and medical services that Hadley has had available to her. He had received no prior medical attention and was suffering greatly from the debilitating effects of Marfan Syndrome. It was yet another opportunity to reflect on how fortunate we were and a humbling reminder that things could always be worse. It was deeply rewarding to see this young man get the help he needed, partly as a result of Hadley's efforts.

Hadley and her brothers also visited the local school, where they assisted with vision screenings. Hundreds of glasses with varying prescriptions had been brought down for children with vision problems. Each would be fitted with a pair that was closest to their needed prescription. Hayden, Hadley, and Griffin interacted with all of these welcoming Hispanic children and also some American children that attended the school. They became quick friends and were even able to go to class with them for part of the day. The parents and staff at the school provided the most incredible spread of authentic Mexican food for lunch, which we all gladly devoured.

Each night, the town put on a special celebration, including delicious food and fabulous entertainment. On the final evening, they put on a Mexican Rodeo with everything from bulls and horses to dancers and mariachi bands. Hadley received a special honor that night from the Mayor of Dublan for her efforts in donating money to help the dear people of this town. I wish I could have bottled the feeling of that night. It was pure joy.

We met so many wonderful people on that trip that radiated love and goodness. Not only was it the delightful people of Dublan but also the doctors that donated their time and talents to help change the lives of others. It was truly an honor to be part of such a noble cause, and we benefitted from the experience as much as those we served. Our family was able to reflect on the bounteous blessings we have in America. It was a trip that forever changed us. This remarkable journey was made possible because of Hadley's Vision.

CHAPTER TEN

Wild Horses

It's often said there is nothing better for the inside of a man than the outside of a horse.

Ronald Reagan

Dad's voice boomed across the horse corral at our family ranch. "Howdy, Partner!" he called. Like one of his well-trained horses, Hadley ran to him, anxious to pick up her training where they had left off.

"You've grown since last week! Pretty soon you'll be able to hit the rim," my dad said affectionately, stroking Hadley's hair as she leaned forward and put her arms around his neck. "Did you see the Suns play yesterday, Grandpa?"

"You know I did! I've got tickets for when they play the Celtics. Do you want to come?"

Magic words.

The ranch in Christopher Creek was my father's favorite place, especially when we were all there as a family. I was a baby when I made my first trip to Ranch 13, and I have watched it expand from a small homestead to a large gathering place for me and my nine brothers and sisters and their families. My private escape is the large wraparound porch overlooking the forest, creek, and lush meadow below. I love to sit in the rocking chair for hours, taking in the view and listening to the birds chirping. It was at this ranch that my dad bonded with each of his grandchildren. Although he was in his sixties, this was the one place he didn't feel his age. At 6'5", Grandpa Barney towered over nearly everyone. When he walked in a room, his presence was felt immediately. But it was not only physical—people were drawn to him. Even the most difficult to love would find a friend in my dad.

Hadley had a special love for Grandpa Barney. They had so much in common. Hadley received not only his height but also his compassion for others—and his penchant for teasing. Together, they made nicknames for everyone, and no one was exempt. (Hadley's personal nickname was "Hadley Date Shake.") Their passion for horses and basketball was hard to match. They were kindred spirits; and whether he liked it or not, Hadley was his sidekick whenever she got the chance.

At our family's mountain ranch, she became his ranch hand, his second in command. She helped him groom the horses, watched him work, and hung on his every word. Grandpa Barney had taken Hadley riding from the time she was a baby. She loved to feel the horse's mane through her fingers as her grandpa galloped through the meadows surrounding the ranch. By the time she was six, she had outgrown the need for a partner and wanted to ride all by herself. She wanted to hold the reigns and explore the many trails that surrounded the ranch. By the time she was twelve, Hadley could round up and saddle the horses herself.

I did not share their passion for riding horses, but on rare occasions I would go on rides with Hadley and my dad. Dad's gentle power of persuasion got most of us up on a horse sooner or later—and Hadley's chiding, "Don't be a wimp," didn't hurt, either.

One day, out on a ride with the two of them, Hadley's horse, a beautiful sorrel horse named Jack, got spooked and darted off, nearly knocking Hadley to the ground.

"Hadley, hold on tight!" I screamed. I watched Hadley rocket straight towards a large branch that threatened to knock her off the horse. The branch hit her squarely in the face and scraped her cheek badly. The horse continued to run at breakneck speed, with Hadley holding on for dear life.

I tried to suppress the memory that seeped into my consciousness. When I was Hadley's age, I backed a horse off a ravine near the ranch house. The horse I was riding, Mighty Rough, began veering off the path. I panicked and began pulling back on the reigns over and over again. I was trying to stop the horse but, in my panic, was actually directing it to go in reverse. The closer I got to the edge of the cliff, the more sure I was that my life would come to an abrupt end. As I watched Hadley, those similar feelings of hysteria began to swell in my throat. But instead of panicking, Hadley listened to her grandpa's voice, following his every direction, calming the horse down. She approached this majestic animal as an equal. I was in awe. And her grandpa was proud.

We knew my father's big heart drew everyone he knew into his life, but no one knew that his heart was so enlarged that his life was at risk.

It was the kids' first day back to school after Christmas break, and they were especially excited to be going to their new school. I had just talked to my dad that morning and had updated him on the kids' first day. He was as excited as I was about the new changes in our life. I was busy getting the house back in order when Yolanda, my parents' housekeeper, called. She was frantic, telling me over and over again my dad wouldn't wake up. It took a moment to register, but then I quickly grabbed Lincoln, loaded him into my car, and rushed to my parents' house, which was about five minutes away. I made the dreaded call to 911. The police and my older brother beat me there. They had moved my dad from his office chair to the entryway floor. Seeing my strong, larger-than-life father laying there lifeless is an image I will never forget. The paramedics arrived shortly after I did. They spent an hour attempting to recover my dad, but to no avail—he was gone. Dad passed away on January 5, 2009, at the young age of 62. It was a day that will be forever seared in our hearts and has left a void that will never be filled. The loss of my dad and Hadley's grandpa has been the single greatest heartache in both of our lives. Hadley explains in the paragraphs that follow.

I couldn't wait for my first day of sixth grade at my new school. We just moved into our new house on Linda Lane, and I was finally going to be able to ride my bike. I also couldn't wait to have a real library and a real cafeteria. I was excited to make new friends at my new school too. I had been going to Challenger Basic School for six and a half years. I was ready for a change!

We were able to live with Grandpa and Grandma Barney while we were remodeling our house. I loved living with them. Every day my grandpa would make us something yummy for breakfast—my favorite was his breakfast burros.

When I would come downstairs to eat, he would say, "Top of the morning!" He was always happy. I had my eleventh birthday while I was living there, and he took me out to breakfast before school. Lincoln, my grandma, and my parents came too. I will never forget that birthday. I didn't know that it would be the last time we would celebrate together.

My grandpa and I would feed the horses together every day. I think I loved horses so much because of him. I always looked forward to spending time with my grandpa; he always made me feel so special. "How's my girl?" he would ask when he came home from work. I knew he loved me, and I loved him.

I was really enjoying my first day at my new school. I had just gotten back from lunch and was sitting at my desk. A call came over the intercom that I needed to come up to the front office. This had never happened before, so I didn't know what it meant. I didn't have a good feeling. When I got up to the front, Grandma Nielson was waiting for me. Griffin and my other cousins at that school had been called out of class too. I was really beginning to worry now. My grandma took me outside, and I could tell she had been crying. I asked her what was wrong. She said we needed to go to Grandpa Barney's house because something was wrong with him. It was about a five-minute drive from my school. When I got there, cars lined the street, and people were everywhere. My mom came outside, and I could see she had been crying too. That is when she told me that my grandpa had passed away. I just screamed, "What? No!" I didn't want to hear it. I began crying too. It couldn't be true. I had just talked to him the day before, and he was fine. Now today while he was sitting in his office chair at home, he fell asleep and never woke up.

I was able to see him one last time at his home. He looked so peaceful. All my family was there, and everyone was crying. It was the worst day of my entire life. I already missed him so much. My life would never be the same without him. I loved my grandpa so much.

We found out later that he died of an enlarged heart. It just stopped working. His heart was just too big, just like mine. I wondered if they could have helped him too, if they would have known.

The time we spend now at the ranch is bittersweet as we reflect on the absence of this great man we love. There is always joy amidst the sadness, because ultimately we know my dad would want us to carry on his dream of working and playing together at the ranch. Whenever I see a full moon, watch a classic Western movie, eat oatmeal raisin cookies, or drive in the car, I remember my amazing dad. With his big stature, big dreams, and big heart, he was an example of a life well lived—and my daughter's hero.

Chapter Eleven

Busy Butterfly

Love is like a butterfly:
It goes wherever it pleases
and pleases wherever it goes.

ANONYMOUS

One of Hadley's most beautiful qualities is her desire to serve. Both the tumultuous course of Hadley's life and the positive influences in her life have allowed her to break through the cocoon of teenage insecurity at an early age and etch out a strong identity essential for focusing on others. Reaching out to serve may have come naturally, but it wasn't always easy.

In junior high school, she got the green light from her doctor to try out for volleyball. This sport did not carry the same potential health hazards as basketball and would still utilize her height advantage. She never acquired the same love for this sport as she did for basketball, but she was willing to give it a try. She had taken a couple of volleyball summer camps, but she was still a beginner. The competition was steep at the junior high level. Over sixty girls tried out, and many had been playing for years at the club level. Talan and I were nervous during this process because while she had the height, she didn't have the experience. Rejection was not something she had faced yet, because she had never really tried out for anything. We were on pins and needles when the day came to find out who made the team. Talan and I were on a trip in Canada, which added to the pressure—we would not be there to cheer for her or to comfort her, depending on the outcome. When we got Hadley's phone call, we were overjoyed. She had made the volleyball team as a developmental player! We didn't know what that meant, but we all cheered with excitement. She was on the team, and that was good enough for us.

Practices began immediately and were rigorous—they were held every day after school and early on Friday mornings. Hadley was extremely committed and worked hard alongside her teammates. It wasn't until her first game we learned what a "developmental player" really was. Basically, it was code for becoming friends with the bench. There were twelve players, and she was number twelve. It was painful to watch her sit game after game playing only briefly on the court.

As the season progressed, it wore on Hadley too. One day toward the end of the school year, she came home in an uncharacteristically solemn mood. Her shoulders were slumped, and she was missing her usual vibrant smile. I knew immediately that something was wrong.

"Mom, the coach invited everyone to lunch except for me!" she blurted, unable to conceal her emotions any longer. Her coach had sought out and personally invited all but two players from the volleyball team for a special end-of-the-year lunch in his office that day. She felt completely embarrassed and ate lunch alone. She had never experienced this type of rejection before, and there was nothing we could do. We could only sit on the sidelines and watch.

Hadley finished out a less-than-stellar season. But she made wonderful friends and even found the courage to try out the following year; fortunately, the next time she was not player twelve but instead an "official" member of the team! We were grateful that she had continued to grow from her struggle and had developed wings strong enough to fly.

Hadley's trials have blessed her with determination and physical strength; but even more importantly, they have given her the ability to handle high school's social scene with a deft hand. Her abilities to deflect rude comments, diffuse awkward social situations with humor, and be kind to others have allowed her to shine socially.

When rude comments are directed towards her, Hadley is astoundingly unaffected. In fact, it seems the more others point out her differences, the more she enjoys emphasizing them. She recently decided to wear her sports goggles to school, drawing even more attention to her appearance; but the more snide comments she received, the more determined she became to wear them. Much to her chagrin, Hadley was required to wear a skirt to school on game days in junior high. When a ruthless boy told her she looked like a man in a skirt, Hadley simply responded, "You just wish you were as tall as me!" He didn't quite know how to respond! Of course, I wanted to wring his neck, but she handled it. Not only did the boy leave her alone, but he and Hadley eventually became friends.

Hadley's experience with Marfan's has required her to search her soul at an early age. Ultimately, Hadley's strength is rooted in her belief that she is a child of

God, and He loves her. She knows she has a purpose in life. From this secure foundation, she has forged an identity all her own, free from the shackles of insecurity. Anchored by the knowledge of her divine worth, she has withstood fierce winds of adversity and has become stronger because of it.

I recently asked Hadley, "If you could change anything, what would it be?" Surprisingly, she didn't answer quickly. I could think of a handful of things off the top of my head that I would change if I could. After a few minutes, she announced, "I wish we wouldn't have done the hormone therapy to stop my growth. I want to be taller." Hadley is over 6'2" tall—and when she is asked her height, she rounds up to 6'3". I thought I was acting in her best interests when we began the hormone therapy, so this came as a shock. In retrospect, it shouldn't have—the day her older brother, Hayden, outgrew her was one of the most disappointing of her life!

Hadley loves herself without an asterisk. Occasionally people treat her with pity. "That poor girl, she is so big. How does she get around?" is one of the many insensitive comments I have heard from adults—but what Hadley understands that others miss is that the qualities that make her exceptionally different are also what make her just plain exceptional. And because she accepts herself, she is able to embrace others for who they are, differences and all.

After we moved to our new house, I was going through Hadley's old schoolwork. I came upon a story she'd written in third grade entitled, "Busy Butterflie":

> *In my backyard I saw a catterpiller and it was looking for food and he ate it. Then the next day later it was in it's cocoon. I came outside and looked on the leef and it was brown. For three weeks I looked at it every day and one day it wasn't there. That's because it came out of its cocoon and I cawt it. I cept it for a cople of days and then I let it go. It stayed in my back yard and I wood feed it tiny peses of bread. I wood play with it and one day it went away. I was happy because there was one reson that it went away, because he was a busy buterflie. That is what he was ment to be.*

I laughed at her spelling mistakes and appreciated how much she'd grown since then. I was struck by how early on Hadley had grasped such mature concepts relating to our purpose in life.

Hadley has continually approached her struggle with Marfan's with optimism and dignity. She has matured physically, socially, and spiritually and has truly become the beautiful young woman she was meant to be. What's more, she opens her heart and helps others grow in the same way. I believe that Hadley's mission on this earth is to teach others about the power of love—how to love ourselves and then love others in return. Hadley may have a severe vision problem, but it is she who sees clearly the things that matter most.

CHAPTER TWELVE

Best Day Ever

When we lose one blessing,
another is often given
most unexpectedly in its place.

C. S. Lewis

Hadley kicked her legs back and forth on the chair, watching the clock. The fluorescent light attached to the ceiling above me buzzed loudly as we waited for the doctor. The stuffy air seemed to stick to the beads of sweat that were bubbling from my pores as I attempted to fan myself with a folded brochure. The doctor's office was more oppressive than usual that day.

My thoughts were interrupted by the soft voice next to me.

"Do you think they will ever invent a cure for Marfan Syndrome?" Hadley wondered aloud.

"That would be amazing, wouldn't it?" I answered with pretend enthusiasm.

I could hardly remember a time when Marfan Syndrome wasn't part of our life. Like a prisoner attached to a ball and chain, I had been dragging Hadley and myself through the muck of endless hospital visits, constant restrictions, and endless worry. I couldn't imagine a world free from it. Marfan Syndrome was the unwelcome member of our family—and wish as we might, there was no disowning it.

The notion of finding a cure for Marfan Syndrome was out of the realm of possibility for Hadley. We had heard the same response, year after year, and knew what the cardiologist would report: "No change. Enlarged heart. Vision problems. Avoid contact sports." We were now accustomed to this and were prepared for the outcome of today's appointment.

My thoughts wandered as I considered what Hadley had sacrificed because of Marfan's. The most difficult sacrifice was that Hadley could not play basketball. For some, this would have been nothing more than an annoyance. But for a determined little girl whose dream was to play for the WNBA, it was a crushing blow. Because of her enlarged heart, contact sports were life threatening. Basketball was out of the question.

Tears filled my eyes as I recalled some of the most recent heartbreaks. Not long after Hadley's diagnosis, a group of neighborhood girls had formed a basketball team and invited Hadley to join in. As if in slow motion, I watched Hadley's eyes sparkle with excitement then fall in disappointment when she realized she wasn't allowed to play. Year after year, the sign-ups for basketball would come around; and each year, we crushed her dreams with a single word: "No." These images played in my mind like an old-fashioned movie reel.

My thoughts were interrupted by the charge nurse. "Hadley Nielson. Are you ready? The doctor wants me to prep you for the EKG."

"I was born ready!" Hadley responded enthusiastically. We walked into the next room, where the nurse slathered her with cold gel and covered her with electrodes. Like the previous six years, Hadley laid down on the padded table while the echocardiogram measured the rhythm of her heart. Then she plodded to the next room, where the tech measured the size of her heart on an ultrasound machine. Finally, Hadley ran on the treadmill while a nurse monitored her heart rate. The familiar procedure ended with another long wait.

Finally, Dr. Martinez walked into the room.

"How have you been feeling, Hadley?" the doctor inquired.

"Fine, I guess," Hadley yawned.

I braced myself for the bleak report we had heard so many times before and fought to calm my nerves.

"I have some news that I think you will be very pleased with," Dr. Martinez offered. "Your aorta is still enlarged, but it is now miraculously in proportion with the rest of your body."

Hadley and I sat in the room with our mouths agape—so stunned that we failed to respond. With an awkward clearing of his throat, Dr. Martinez continued.

"As I am guessing by your response, you know that this is highly unusual. In fact, it's nothing short of a miracle." Dr. Martinez paused, suddenly realizing the importance of his next words to this little girl. "After careful consideration, I feel it is safe to remove the contact sports restriction."

Again, silence filled the room as our eyes grew moist. I gathered the courage to ask the burning question. "Does this mean she can play basketball?"

"Yes, that's correct."

With those words of affirmation, the floodgates opened. Hadley and I started jumping up and down, bursting with tears and shouts of joy. We even dragged the good doctor into the exuberance as we laughed, cried, and gave thanks to God for providing us with a miracle. Hadley's words described it perfectly:

> *When I thought all was lost, the doctor told me the news I will never forget—I was now allowed to play basketball! That was probably the best moment and will be the best moment of my entire life. Ever since that day, I have been working my tail off to get there . . . to the WNBA.*

Six years earlier, Hadley received the devastating diagnosis of Marfan Syndrome. It turned her life upside down and threatened to crush her spirit. But like a flower that breaks through the barren ground, Hadley's indomitable spirit fought back, becoming even more beautiful from the scorching trials, torrential downpour of disappointment, and chilling heartache she was forced to endure. She thrived—and lifted all of us up in the process.

Epilogue

Reach high, for stars are hidden in your soul. Dream deep, for every dream precedes the goal.

MOTHER TERESA

So much of life is still to come for our brown-eyed girl, Hadley. Sports will no doubt be a large part of whatever her future holds. Basketball is her passion; and aside from school, church, and family, it is the biggest part of her life. This is a passion that she shares with her dad and brothers; and once she got the green light from her doctor, she was off like a racehorse.

Hadley has to compensate for some Marfan-related physical challenges. She has to work extra hard to gain strength and agility. She has grown so tall so fast that her coordination is just now catching up with her. Her visual impairment is also severe. Watching Hadley miss a simple basketball pass or struggle to read a playbook with her nose almost to the page is a heartbreaking reminder of how bad her vision really is. Hadley never lets on, but if you watch her closely it becomes painfully clear. Talan wants to have a pair of glasses made so that the rest of us—coaches included—can see things from Hadley's perspective.

Hadley's height, wingspan, determination, and natural talent more than make up for the challenges she faces playing basketball. When people with Marfan Syndrome stretch out their arms, the length of their arms is much greater than their height. Her wingspan of 6'5" allows her to reach farther, higher, and wider than any of her teammates. This, combined with her height, gives Hadley a distinct advantage over her opponents. Besides her physical advantages, Hadley works diligently to achieve her goals. Her motto is, "Practice doesn't make perfect. Perfect practice makes perfect." When she's not working or going to school, you'll find her outside shooting baskets or analyzing a recent WNBA game on ESPN. Hard work is the key to her success in basketball and everything else she pursues. Hadley was awarded the MVP for her eighth grade basketball team and then went on to be the team captain of her high school team the following year. She was the MVP that year as well. These honors have only fed her hunger to shoot better, reach farther, jump higher, and run faster.

Hadley's story is still being written. She is not a perfect person, but she has perfected many qualities that make her a person worth emulating. She has plans to make humanitarian trips to Africa and, of course, play in the WNBA. For now, though, she is doing what she loves most—playing basketball. While she will always battle with her health, and doctor's appointments will never cease, Hadley forges ahead, living her life to the fullest and making the most of what she has been given. Talan and I are both vying for the title of Hadley's biggest fan, and we are elated that she is now on the road to fulfilling her lifelong dream. Our rubber band girl brings light and love to everyone around her as she joyfully lives "happily ever after" every day of her life.

ACKNOWLEDGMENTS

And whatsoever ye do,
do it heartily.

COLOSSIANS 3:23

To begin, I must first give a profound and sincere thank you to my dear friend of nearly thirty years, Cara Hadley Cragun. Without her, this book simply never would have been written. We were sitting on the beach together when the idea for *Rubber Band Girl* was born. She gave me the support I needed to take on this project and soon became my cheerleader and sounding board. Cara was instrumental in leading me to my publisher, Amy Cook, who is one of the most intelligent, talented, and kindhearted people I know. She gave me the reigns to this project but always knew when to pull back and managed to push me in ways I have never been pushed. I am so thankful to her for believing in me. Thank you also to my editor, Jennifer Cummings, who put the cherry on the sundae in editing the book. She is amazing!

I also want to express my heartfelt appreciation to my family and friends for reading the book as it developed, offering constructive criticism when needed, and, most importantly, giving me kind words of encouragement. It seemed that every idea offered was a necessary catalyst for adding an important angle to the book. Thanks to my mom, who passed along her perfectionist gene—it was essential for writing this book. I love you, Mom!

Thank you to another lifelong friend, Tracey Simas, for her photography skills. She did a fabulous job capturing the unique bond between Hadley and me while making us look amazing in the process. She is truly gifted! Thank you also to Claire B. Cotts for answering an email from an unknown author. When I saw her artwork displayed at Nordstrom, I immediately fell in love with her style and hoped she would be willing to take on this little project. She was gracious enough to agree and contributed her extraordinary talent to create an incredible piece of art for the cover of *Rubber Band Girl.*

I always love to save the best for last. My deepest thanks go to my precious husband, Talan, and five children, Hayden, Hadley, Griffin, Lincoln, and Clover, for allowing their wife and mom to do what was necessary to write this book. Many nights, I started writing as they went to sleep and continued until the sun rose the next morning. They often woke up to their mom typing away at the computer, which usually meant one thing—cold cereal for breakfast! They all pitched in to fill in the gaps and were extremely loving and supportive during this exhausting process.

To my darling daughter, Hadley, thank you for teaching me that anything is possible! You have shown me that many of the limits we have in life are self-imposed. Because of you, I had the courage to tackle what seemed to be a daunting and nearly impossible task. Thank you, Hadley, for living a life that has touched me and taught me life lessons that I would not have otherwise learned. Remember, you are still my little girl—no matter how tall you are! I love you deeply, forever and always.